Sparkle OF HIS EYE

BY: C. KELLY

D1519768

Printed in the United States of America

First Printing, 2017

ISBN-13:
978-1544887470

ISBN-10:
1544887477

Introduction

"Beat that bitch ass Keisha!" Tiffany yelled from the bathroom door. They were supposed to be in their third period math class, but as soon as Tiffany saw Ebony walking towards the bathroom she had to tell her girl Keisha. Keisha kept raining punches on Ebony's face.

"Bitch you was all talk in front of yo' friends, talk that hot shit now." Keisha said as she continued to make Ebony her punching bag. Ebony tried her best to fight back, but it was no use because all her swinging couldn't stop Keisha. See Keisha and Ebony use to be thick as thieves, that is until Ebony was caught face down ass up with Keisha's boyfriend Jason. Ever since then it's been fight on sight for Keisha when it came to Ebony's ass. And Ebony knew it.

"Aight boo let's go! Here comes Ms. Williams! We gotta go! You know she hates my ass." Tiffany couldn't stand Ms. Williams the English teacher because she always had some smartass comments to make about Tiffany and her girls. Sasha and Tiffany walked out the bathroom and pass Ms. Williams as if nothing had happened.

"Shouldn't y'all fast tails be in class or do I need to write both of you up for skipping?" Ms. Williams asked when she spotted us sneaking away from the scene.

"Nah, we are just coming from the office headed back to class now." Keisha said while giving Ms. Williams the fakest smile she could come up with. As they walked into their math class the bell rang signaling that class was over. Though they had missed the class, they didn't give it much of a second thought. Keisha and Tiffany were both seniors and had just a few weeks left before they would be graduating, and a write up.

"I can't stand that fat bitch. She always talkin' out the side of her fuckin' face." Tiffany snapped bitterly as she grabbed her books off her desk, and headed back out the class.

"What's poppin' bitches!" Sparkle yelled as Keisha and Tiffany walked out of their class and joined her in the hallway. "Bitch you just missed it! I just saw Ebony running out of the school, and it looked like she got her ass tagged by a room full of big bitches." Sparkle was laughing so hard as she told her girls what she saw. That was one thing about Sparkle, she told everything she saw, or heard. Nobody tried to check her though because she had hands for days, and didn't mind beating a bitch down if they stepped to her. If a nigga tried to pop slick she had three crazy ass brothers who would fill any nigga walking with lead about their baby sister. Keisha and Tiffany looked at her and bust out laughing.

"Oh we saw her alright. Keisha blessed that bitch with them hands." Tiffany stated while continuing to laugh.

"Well damn one of you hoes could have told me."

"Calm down Spark, Tiffany saw the hoe walking to the bathroom, and I went to handle that. No big deal, now let's go eat cause I'm starving."

Keisha could eat, but all her weight was in the right places. She was an eighteen-year old but was built like Buffy the Body. Most of the kids around the school compared her looks to the actress Meagan Good. She knew she was the shit and made sure to remind whoever felt the need to say otherwise.

"Damn Ma what's good? You can't speak no more?"

"Man Jason get out of my face. I told you I'm not messing with you no more and I mean that. You need to call your bitch

Ebony."

"Okay cool, I see you playing tough around your clique. I guess I will see you tonight at Chris's party." Jason knew he fucked up by smashing Ebony, but she kept throwing the pussy at him so he gave her what she wanted. To him it was just a fuck but it was clear that Keisha saw it totally different.

"Speaking of Chris's party, what are we going to wear?" Sparkle always stressed over what to wear as if she didn't have shit that would shut down the scene once she made her entrance. She was short, light skinned and what most people would call *Slim Thick*. She swore up and down that Fetty Wap made that song about her, and you couldn't tell her any different. She had long hair that stopped at her waist and looked just like the singer Aaliyah.

Tiffany was just as bad as her two friends. She wasn't the thickest but far from the smallest. She had ass and titties for days. Tiffany was light brown, and rocked the hell out of her pixie cut. Needless to say, they were three of the baddest chicks walking the streets of the Lou, and that's where they got the name, the Thick Dime Pieces, from.

Whenever they walked in a room together everyone showed

them love. The TDPs were known for their Instagram pictures and turning up at all the local parties. Don't get it twisted though, they were far more than pretty faces and fat asses. They had goals and dreams of getting out of the hood and making it on to something better. While most people showed them love there was still the handful that managed to hate on them and it didn't go unnoticed.

Chapter 1: Sparkle

As soon as we pulled up to the street we had a hard time finding a parking spot. My bitches were already turnt and still pregaming before we finally found a spot to park.

"Pass me the blunt Tiffany. Damn you act like you the only bitch smoking tonight."

I wasn't a smoker but I did hit the blunt on occasions. I was a drinker and it didn't matter if it was dark or light, if it was liquoring I was downing it.

"Aye! This my shit!" Keisha yelled before she started shaking her ass to the song.

"Hey, let's take a picture for the 'Gram before we go in." I had on a black bodycon dress from Bebe, black and gold heels with gold accessories to match. My hair was bone straight with a part down the middle. While most of these birds were walking around paying hundreds for bundles my shit was real and I took pride in my hair.

"Hurry up and snap the picture, I'm ready to turn the fuck up." I looked at the picture and all of my thoughts were confirmed I was the baddest bitch. I logged into Instagram, and posted the picture with the caption *Pretty on Fleek #Slimthick*.

When we walked in the party the DJ got on the mic and yelled "TDPs in the motherfucking building!"

I'm with some hood girls lookin' back at it

And a good girl in my tax bracket

Got a black card that let sacs have it

These Chanel bags is a bad habit

Nicki Minaj's *Feelin' Myself* was blasting through the speakers and I was definitely feeling myself.

"Ay Spark, I'll be back, Jason ass keeps texting me telling me to meet him outside."

"Cool, girl be careful though you know I don't trust that lame ass nigga." I couldn't stand Jason from day one. He was good looking but he felt he could do my friend any kind of way. The nigga was fucking any and everything walking. Hell, he was the reason why we don't fuck with Ebony anymore. Don't get me wrong what happened was between them three, but I feel like if you can fuck your friend's man you can't be trusted.

One thing about the TDPs was were weren't hoes and Ebony was far from a nun. The bitch had so many bodies that she could have her own cemetery. Please don't think I'm a saint cause that would be a damn lie. I've done my dress and I dress very revealing, drink like a damn fish, and would beat a bitch ass in a New York minute but I didn't open my legs to any and every nigga. To be quite frank my legs have never been open for any nigga. I was saving myself for that special one.

I turned my head and Tiff was twerking all over some fine ass dude. I decided to go get a drink since I didn't want to sweat my hair out dancing too long. While I was pouring myself a cup of Remy, I just kept thinking about how I was going to tell my friends I couldn't be kicking it with them as much until after graduation.

I still haven't gotten a letter from Wash U and that was weighing heavy on me. I needed to get into this school because I didn't apply to any other colleges. I was banking on my grades getting me the acceptance letter I needed but truthfully, I should have heard something by now.

"What's up sexy?" Those words instantly brought me out off

my daydream. Standing before me was one of the sexiest dude I have seen in a long time. He was at least 6'1 and his low-cut hair had waves for days. He had on a pair of dark Levis with a red Polo shirt, and some red and white J's.

"Hi," was all I could get out. His sexiness had me at a loss for words.

"What's your name ma?"

"Sparkle, but everyone calls me Spark. What's your name?" I was trying my hardest to control the smile that was forcing its way out.

"Everybody calls me Q."

"Well Q, nice to meet you." I said as I stuck out my hand for him to shake. Instead of shaking my hand, he grabbed it and kissed it before flashing me a huge, perfect smile. He held on to my hand and pulled me close enough to take a good, long whiff of his cologne. Guilty Gucci. This dude knew just what to do to make a bitch fall for him, and it was working.

"Can I get a dance Sparkle?"

Before I could respond I felt my phone vibrating. I looked down, it was a text from Tiffany.

Tiff: Yasss Bish Yasss. He is sexy as fuck! You better work

I damn near fell out laughing. Tiffany knew she was a damn fool. I looked around the party for her and I saw her crazy ass making all kinds of goofy faces at me from a corner in the room not too far away from where I stood while entertaining the same dude from earlier. I just shook my head.

"So can I get that dance or was that your dude telling you to get home?"

"Actually, that was my bestfriend and sure we can dance." We walked to the center of the room, and I started dancing for him like he was the only other person in the room with me.

Boy, I'm drinking, I'm singing

"Damn ma that shit sexy as fuck," Q said as I twirled my ass in front of him along to the sounds of Beyonce's hit *Drunk in Love*. I looked over my shoulder and smiled while I continued to give him a show. Out the corner of my eye I saw Ebony standing with a few chicks. Usually I wouldn't pay the hoe no attention but what really caught my attention was how one of them was basically eye fucking me. She had the nerves to roll her eyes at me as if she wasn't just staring me down. I kept dancing until the song went off, then Q grabbed my hand and pulled me to a corner. While he admired my body I pulled my phone out to snap some more pictures of myself.

"Can I call you later?" He asked as I snapped another picture.

"Yeah I think we can make that happen." I said as I grabbed his phone and put my number in it. One thing I loved was a man that knew what he wanted and went for it. When I handed it back to him he started messing with his phone. Instantly mine started vibrating again letting me know I had a call.

"That's my number lock me in." He said before pressing end.

"Before I go let's take a picture since you seem to like doing that so much." he offered, snatching my phone out of my hand and pulled me in for the picture. He wrapped his arm around my waist and kissed me on my cheek as he snapped the picture. Feeling the warmness of his body so close to mine had me wondering exactly what I was missing out on by not having sex. My gut was telling me that Q was going to be the one that showed me, and boy was I ready. Once we were done taking the picture he started typing something into my phone before he handed it back, but before I could see what he was doing the girl that was eye fucking me was in Q's face.

"Are you really going to disrespect me like I'm not here? You kissing, and grinding all over this chick like you don't see me." It was clear from the way she was acting that they had some sort of bond, and I was not about to have my name ringing in these streets as a hoe.

"Um yeah I see you have a situation so I'm going to let you handle that." I said as I walked away from the two of them. As soon as I walked over to Tiffany, Keisha walked up and she was clearly pissed.

"I'm ready to go!" She yelled over the music. I was ready to leave myself. As bad as I wanted to look over in the direction of mister right I just couldn't bring myself to do so. Just when I though I found a little "friend" it turns out he was already taken. My girls and I walked through the dimly lit basement, and up the stairs to make our departure. The entire drive to take Keisha, and Tiffany home was a quiet trip. Both of my friends were clearly wrapped up in their own thoughts, and I couldn't take my mind off Q.

After I dropped Tiff and Keisha off, I hurried up and got

home so that I could get to sleep. It was already after 2:00 0am and I was done for. I quietly snuck in the house making sure not to close the front door too loud because the last thing I wanted to do was wake up my mom. She would have a whole damn fit if she knew I was just getting in.

Even though I was eighteen she didn't play that staying out all night shit. Creeping through the dark house was something that I have done plenty of times, but I knew I couldn't keep making this a habit. My plan is to buy me a condo as soon as I graduate high school. I made it to my room and closed my door. Thank God I had a bathroom in my room because I did not want to hear her mouth about anything tonight. I took a shower and hopped in bed.

Before I could even close my eyes my phone was doing numbers. I looked at it, and seen I had four text from Tiffany, Keisha, and my manager Alex. I also had a bunch of Instagram notifications which was nothing new to me but the amount was a little different. I decided to look at those first since I could just about guess what my text were about. To my surprise, I saw the picture that Q and I took, swooning happily at the results.

Not only did I think it was cute but clearly my fans did too

SPARKLE OF HIS EYE

because the post already had 200+ likes and over twenty comments. The caption read *My Future Wifey #BaddestBitch.* He even tagged himself to the photo. I decided to read some of the comments.

Most were people saying we were a cute couple, or asking him who I was. The comment that caught my eye was some chick name *cookies_cream95.* She had the nerves to say the picture was ugly. Clearly she was hating 'cause wasn't shit about the picture ugly. I chose not to respond because I didn't need the unnecessary drama.

Next I decided to read my text. I had one from Tiffany letting me know she was coming over tomorrow so we could chill. I had one from Keisha that simply read *Ugh......I hate his ass!* I shook my head cause I knew that she was going to cave in to Jason the first chance he got her alone. Then I noticed two from an unknown number. It read:

(555)339-7208: R u woke

(555)339-7208: ???

I was so confused because I didn't know who would be

asking me if I was woke. So, I replied *Yes*.

Thinking nothing of it I put my phone on my nightstand and turned over to go to sleep. As soon as my head hit my pillow my phone started going off again. I grabbed it without looking at the screen. "Hello?"

"My bad, you sound sleep. I can call you back tomorrow if you want," the voice on the other end spoke.

His voice made me hot between my thighs. I instantly sat up, and looked at the screen.

"Who is this?" Deep in the pit of my stomach I knew it was Q, but I wasn't expecting him to sound this damn sexy on the phone. He officially had the total package in my eyes.

"Q, but since you are asking I know you didn't lock my number in."

I can't believe this nigga had some nerves to be calling me after his girlfriend just confronted him for chilling with me at the party.

"Are you sure you dialed the right number because I would hate for you chick to hear you talking to me. Look Q you cool and all, but I don't play sideline to anybody, and I'm not about to start." I needed to set the record straight up front so that he wouldn't try to play me. I would hate to have my brothers kick his ass for hurting me.

"Chill ma that's why I called you. She ain't my girl. She's a bitter ex." The way he raised his voice to shut me up had my panties instantly wet.

"Just a bitter ex huh?" He could run that line on these other simple chicks, but I wasn't buying it.

"Well actually she's my baby mama Brittany. And before you even ask, no we not together and haven't been together since she was pregnant with my seed. She was on some childish ass shit tonight, dead ass. Now that you know all that, I'm trying to get to know you better. So what's up?"

Baby mama? Seed? Was I hearing this nigga correctly?

"So what you are saying is little Ms Brittany is your baby mama, but y'all don't fuck? How old is your baby? Wait how old are you?" To say I was beyond done was an understatement. One thing I didn't do was the baby mama drama and I already had it just from one dance and a picture.

"Slow down with all the questions. I'm twenty-two, and yes

she is my baby's mother. My daughter is eight months old, and she is my world. I just can't stand the person I created her with. Now that you know about me tell me something about yourself." I told him my age, and that I was a senior at Sumner about to graduate. We talked for another hour or so about my goals and he felt he could be apart of those goals. He told me he was an entrepreneur, and he pictured me as his wife carrying his next child. The conversation continued like that for a while longer before I told him I was about to call it a night. I did however agree to see him tomorrow so that we could finish our conversation in person.

The next morning I woke up to Tiffany and Sasha flopping down on my bed. "Damn bitch don't sleep your life away, get up." Keisha said with much attitude.

"Good morning to you too rude bitch. The least you could do when you wake me up is leave the attitude at the door." I said as I got up, and headed to my bathroom to brush my teeth, and wash my face.

"Whatever hoe, and it's not morning. It's after two, and yo ass laying in here like a damn zombie. Oh, and what's good with that picture you put on the Gram?" Keisha was never the type to sugarcoat how she felt, and it rubbed me the wrong way at times.

"First off I didn't put that picture on there, Q did. Secondly, we were on the phone for over an hour after I came home last night. That's why I was still asleep," I stated matter-of-factly. I sat back on my bed and began to tell my friends how Q believed we were going to get married, and how he envisioned me carrying his child. One thing I was bad at was hiding how I felt because my facial expressions always gave me away, and this time was no different. The smile I was wearing could be seen through a thick cloud of fog.

"Y'all I'm really feeling Q. His voice is so intoxicating and the way he was so sure of himself is a major turn on for me. Not to mention we look good together." Q was like a breath of fresh air for me. I never had a guy come into my life, and make me feel like I was more than just a pretty face.

I mean knew how to hold a conversation without talking about sex, and he actually had a job. Keisha told us about how she was about to forgive Rodney at the party, until some pregnant chick walked up to him calling him her baby daddy. I wanted so badly to say told you so, but I knew my girl was hurting so I kept that comment to myself. Tiffany told us about the dude she met at the party named Nick, and how they hit it off. My phone alerted me that I had a text message, so I grabbed it, and opened the message.

Q(2:21): Good afternoon beautiful. Did you sleep well?

I smiled so damn hard it felt like my face was going to break. I looked at the message again before I decided to respond.

Me(2:23): Hello! Yes up until I was rudely awakened lol

Q(2:24): So can I still see you today?

Me(2:25) Sure what did you have in mind?

Q(2:27) Meet me in twenty minutes at Froyo in the Loop.

Instead of responding I hopped up, and ran to my closet to find something to wear. Thank God I took a shower when I got home last night.

"Damn bitch slow down. What are you rushing for?" Tiffany asked me as I made my way to the closet.

"Girl that was Q, and he wants to meet up now in the Loop." I grabbed a teal loose fitting sundress, and some white Michael Kors sandals, and slid them on. I pulled my hair up into a messy bun, and put on a pair of Ray Ban aviators. I snatched my purse, phone, and keys off my nightstand and left my room. Before we could even get to the front door my mama was on my ass.

"And where do you think you're going? Your mail is on the kitchen counter" My mom hated how I got my money so whenever she saw me heading out she just assumed I was doing something that related to Instagram. Everything I did she made sure to critique. She saw me posting pictures of myself on Instagram as degrading, and a lack of self-respect. She didn't care if it was a picture of a new weave install, or a swimsuit picture. In her eyes, I was selling myself short for money and she couldn't stand it.

Even though we lived in the Ville neighborhood our lifestyle was different from most of the other people in the community. The Ville isn't one of the nicest neighborhoods in St. Louis. Actually, it is an area with very high crime rates, and gang activity. The house we live in is an inheritance from my grandparents, and my mom refused to move because of the crime activity. My mom is a nurse, and ever since my dad divorced my mom and left he has been sending her fat ass checks, and keeping my bank account fed so in her eyes there was no reason I should be doing anything that didn't involve using my brain to make money.

When it came to my dad he traveled a lot because of his profession so he sent money every month to my mom to make sure she didn't have to spend her own, and of course he spoiled me because I was his only daughter.

"I'm headed to the Delmar Loop to get some Froyo I will be back soon. What kind of mail was it ma?"

"Hell, I don't know Sparkle. If you want to know go look at it." My mother was so damn nosey so I knew she looked at the mail, but she was just being a bitch to spite me.

"Whatever ma, I will look at it when I get back, love you." I didn't have time to keep standing there going back and forth with her. I had somewhere I needed to be. Tiffany, Keisha and I hopped in my 2015 Nissan Maxima. My car was my baby. It was all black with black leather interior, and pink stitching. I had some all black rims on it also. I didn't work a traditional nine to five like most teens my age. Me and my bitches were getting that shmoney from sponsors on Instagram, and hosting local parties. I was making at least ten bands a month from my looks alone.

Once we got to the Loop we parked behind Bubble Tea and walked around. The Loop was the go to spot for everybody and their mamas in St. Louis. It was over two city blocks along Delmar that housed different boutiques, shoe stores, restaurants, bars, and other businesses. As soon as we got in front of Froyo Tiffany acted as if she was going to have a damn heart attack. Her dramatic ass was fanning, and throwing her head back.

"Breathe bitch, what's wrong? Are you okay?" Keisha was fanning Tiffany, and trying to figure out what was going on all at once.

"I think I'm pregnant just from looking at his sexy ass. Tiffany exclaimed as she pointed towards the dude she was chilling with last night at the party. The death stare Keisha gave Tiffany spoke volumes, and if looks could kill well let's just say we would be wearing Tiffany's picture on a shirt.

"I should smack your extra ass. I really thought something was wrong with you." Keisha said as we all started laughing.

"Stop playing, and come on so I can see my future baby daddy." My mind was made up, and I was going to make Q my mister if he kept playing his cards right, and saying everything I want to hear.

Chapter 2: Sparkle

Stepping into Froyo I had to admit ol boy Nick was fine. I noticed he was standing next to Q and two other dudes who looked like they had just stepped off the cover of GQ magazine.

"What's up baby girl? You looking nice today." Q knew just what to say to having me blushing. He wrapped his hands around my waist and cupped my ass. I took this time to take in his smell which I noticed was Acqua Di Gio by Giorgio Armani. Not to mention the grip he had on my ass had me wanting to wrap my legs around him, and fuck him right there.

"Thanks, you don't look so bad yourself." I whispered in his ear while wrapping my arms around his neck, and giving him a kiss on the cheek. I released my hold on him, and introduced him and his boys to Tiffany, and Keisha. He did the same and introduced us to his right-hand man Nick, and his younger twin brothers Roderick and Robert.

"Wait y'all play basketball for Vashon."Keisha said remembering their faces. She loved dudes that played sports, but unlike Tiffany who loved older guys Keisha was into dudes our age. There was always some sort of athlete in her DM, but in her mind the were like old men. So it didn't surprise me that she knew who the twins were.

"Yeah that's us, and y'all are the TDPs right?" Q's brother Robert asked.

"Yep that's us in the flesh." Tiffany loved when people mentioned our clique. To her we were royalty, but truth be told we were nowhere near famous.

"Yeah y'all hosted one of our homeboy's party a few weeks ago at the Rustic Goat. That joint was poppin." It was cool that we got recognized by people all the time, but when I wanted to just kick back and chill I didn't want to hear about TDP's or parties. I guess you can say that was one of the downsides to doing what we did for a living.

"Yeah well that was business, and this is pleasure." I stated as I grabbed Q's hand and walked out of Froyo. As we walked we picked up our conversation from the night before.

"So, Sparkle when do you plan on letting me take you out on a real date? We could see a movie, and grab some food afterwards.

or we could watch Netflix and chill." Even though he looked like he was serious I just couldn't pull myself to trust him. Don't get me wrong he hadn't done anything so far to make me not trust him, but seeing the stuff Keisha was going through had me feeling like all dudes talk a good game just to get what they want, and then they dog you out.

"As soon as you decide on a day and time I'm all up for it. Just don't think you are going to hit on the first night cause I'm not that type of girl." He looked at me and smiled as if I had said something funny, but I was dead ass.

"Chill with all that hot shit man. If I wanted to just fuck I would have asked when you were going to let me hit. I'm not one of these lame ass niggas you are used to messing with baby girl." One thing for sure I loved the way he handled me. Most females would be offended by a man talking to them the way he called himself talking to me, but that for me that was a straight panty wetter.

"I didn't say that's all you wanted, but I was making it clear that that isn't what I'm about. So, Quentin what type of work do you do exactly?"

"I own a towing company, and I have another business

venture that I'm into. Does that meet your qualifications?"

"Look Q if you aren't selling drugs, and in a gang then we are cool. I don't have time to be getting shot because I'm with you."

"So, Sparkle do you have a bunch of niggas I need to be worried about, or a crazy boyfriend lurking in the cut because I don't want to have to shoot a nigga?"

"Nope I'm single as a dollar bill. Besides most dudes can't handle what I do for a living."

"Good cause I play for keeps, and I can't have my woman talking to other niggas."

"Who said I wanted to be your woman? I mean I like to do as I please when I please, and having a boyfriend will only slow that down."

"I can see it in your eyes that you want me so you should just stop frontin like you don't want to be seen on my arm. Not only that I want you, and I get what I want." Before I could respond to his comment his phone started ringing. He looked over at me and winked as we continued to walk until his phone rang again. He kept pressing ignore so I knew it was some bird calling because she refused to accept that he wasn't answering and she kept calling. I can't lie though at first I was jealous, but then I remembered I was there with him, and not whoever wanted his attention now.

When his phone went off again I told him to answer it so that we could finish our mini date without further interruptions. I stood off to the side as I heard him arguing with whoever was on the other end. I decided to text Tiffany and told her to meet us in front of Footlocker. When I looked up Q was watching me, and had finished with his call. He pulled me into him, and gave me a kiss on the forehead. As we walked inside of Footlocker I felt as if someone was watching me so I looked around, and there little Ms. Brittany stood on the other side of the store with none other than Ebony, and some other broke down looking bird. At that moment, I was so happy I told Tiffany to meet us here cause if these hoes tried anything they was going to get fucked up.

I turned my attention back to Q, who had continued to look at the new J's that were just released. I was more of a heels type of chick, but when some hot kicks dropped I always copped them. I asked the sales associate if they had them in a size 71/2 and Q asked for them in an 11. While we waited, Q kept telling me jokes, and of course as the goofy chick I am I laughed at them. I guess that got under Brittany's skin cause next thing I know she was in his face again with her minions right behind her.

"What's good Ebony?" I asked trying to stay out of Q's drama with his baby mama. Just like the scary bitch that she is, she didn't say shit. She just turned her head and acted as if she didn't hear me talking to her. As I turned my attention back to Q I heard Brittany trying to go off on Q.

"So, Q you are here with the same chick from the party, but you swore up and down that you don't fuck with her. You full of shit I swear you got me fucked all the way up." The way Brittany was talking it was clear to me that they had more than a co-parenting relationship. Brittany wasn't an ugly girl. She was about five feet three like me. She had chestnut colored skin with pretty brown eyes. Looking at her I wanted to feel sorry for her because she had tears watering up in her eyes, but her mouth wouldn't allow me to feel sorry for her. I just stood there and watched as she had her right hand on her hip, and waved her finger in his face as she talked.

"Man, Brittany gone with all that bullshit you talking." I heard Q say as I turned my attention back to him. He looked as if he wanted to slap her for causing a scene, but he stayed calm. By this point there started to be a crowd of bystanders watching, and pulling out their phones. The last thing I wanted was to see myself on somebody's Facebook live because I was in the middle of this mess. People loved to record other people fighting, and they were even quicker to post it on social media.

"Oh, so since you're entertaining this knock off Aaliyah you wanna try to diss me?" Before I could fix my mouth to say anything Tiffany punched Brittany in the face. Just as Tiffany was about to swing again Brittany recovered from the hit and had pounced on Tiffany. They were going blow for blow, and no one was trying to breaking them up. People had started standing on the benches recording the fight, and I stood off to the side to make sure none of her friends jumped in.

"Ebony if I were you I would just walk away cause I'm tired of beating your ass." Keisha said as she took off her earrings. At this point I was over the whole situation, and hadn't even noticed that Keisha was standing next to me until she said something to Ebony. Me and Q wasn't even together, and I was dealing with his ignorant baby mama. Two big husky white men came running from the back of the store, and prying pulling the two girls apart. Tiffany started throwing display shoes in Brittany's direction as the man holding her tried to get her to calm down.

"Bitch don't get mad at my friend cause your nigga wants her, and not your dusty ass!" The sales associate had finally released Tiffany from his hold he had on her, and Tiffany tried her hardest to straighten her hair up that was now all over her head. She now had a cut on her lip, and her shirt was ripped.

"Naw bitch she don't have him, but I will see yo tired ass again." Brittany said as the associate that was holding her had also let her go, and asked her and her friends to leave the store before we did. As Brittany and her friends walked out of Footlocker she turned around and winked in my direction.

"Q I will deal with you when you get home." The crowd that had formed around us started to slowing go back to shopping, or walking off talking about what had just took place. I turned my attention to Q and slapped the shit out of him.

"So, she's just your baby mama that you don't fuck right, but y'all live together. Nigga you must take me as a fucking fool! Lose my number!" I yelled as me and my girls left the store. He grabbed my arm, but a quickly yanked away. I was so embarrassed the only thing I wanted to do was get the hell away from him, and everybody else.

I swear it felt like I ran to my car how fast I got there. I was too mad I was opening up to this nigga just for him to lie to me. He could have kept it one hundred with me because the way I saw it we barely knew each other so lying wasn't even necessary. It's not like we were fucking or anything. The whole drive back to my house Q kept blowing my line up. I just kept ignoring his calls. I guess he thought that I would read his text, but he was sadly mistaken. I deleted them without even opening them.

When we got back to my house we sat on the porch for a while and talked. I felt I needed to tell my girls I had to fall back on partying until after graduation. I knew they would feel some type of way because partying was how we got paid, but I needed to focus on school, and figure out my next move. Washington University or Wash U for short is a very prestigious school, and being accepted there was the only thing I dreamed about as a child.

"So y'all know how I applied for Wash U right? Well I still haven't heard from them, and to make matters worse my Science grade has dropped. I can't do anymore parties until after graduation because I have to get myself together. I know y'all gone feel some type of way, but y'all already got y'all acceptance letters for UMSL so y'all straight, but for me that was the only school I applied for, and a bitch is straight stressing. "They both looked at me like I was crazy. One thing I knew about my friends they wanted to see me doing well, and I wanted the same for my friends.

"Aww boo, we not mad. I mean I'm going to miss shaking my ass with you for the next couple of weeks, but we understand." Keisha always had to say something about shaking her ass. That was my bitch though. Tiffany just nodded her head in agreement with Sasha. I mentally felt drained. One minute I was concerned about my education and the next minute it seemed as if my personal life was in shambles.

"Well I'm about to take a nap. I'll holla at y'all tomorrow." I was still hungover, and tired from not getting enough sleep. I was still very pissed too. I went straight to my room, fell across the bed and went to sleep.

I was awakened out of my sleep yet again by my damn phone. I had so many missed calls, and text. I decided to just clear my notification screen, and take a shower.

Once I got out of the shower I threw on a pair of shorts and a tank top and headed straight to the kitchen. I was so hungry. It never failed that I always feel like I'm starving whenever I'm going through something. I was an emotional eater at its best. Thank God my mom always cooked before she went to work, or I would have been shit out of luck because I wasn't about to cook a damn thing. I made me a plate of food and sat down at the counter to eat.

Flipping through the mail I saw I had a large envelop from Washington University. I quickly opened it, and the tears began to fall. This was what I had been waiting on. I snatched my phone off the counter and called my mom.

"Ma I got accepted into Wash U.!" I was so happy I didn't even realize I was screaming. "I'm proud of you baby, but I have to get back to work. The food is in the oven, and if you go out tonight make sure you have your ass home at a decent hour tonight Sparkle. Don't think I didn't notice what time you came in last night. "I shook my head at the phone because I really did think she went to sleep early last night. Her ass needed to get a man so that she could take some of her focus off me.

"Bye ma talk to you later." I hurried up off the phone and clicked on my group text. My excitement was through the roof. I had just accomplished the most important thing ever in my whole eighteen years on this earth.

Me: Fuck all that shit I was talking earlier. Let's go to Applebee's for some food, and drinks. Robin bartending tonight so we won't get carded.

Robin was my older cousin from my dad's side, and we were very close. She had been working at Applebee's since she was nineteen, and that's been three years. Three years of underage drinking to say the least.

Keisha: Ayeee! Turn up turn up Turn up!!!! Meet you there in an hour

Tiffany: I'm with Nick, but we down. See you soon besties!

I wanted to ask Tiffany why she was with Nick, but I know that what happened today had nothing to do with either of them. Besides Satan himself could walk in that bitch and I would still be happy. I went in my room found an olive green spandex romper. I lotioned my body down, and slid in it. I threw on a pair of low top white converses, and grabbed my purse and keys, and headed out the door.

As soon as I made it to Applebee's I could tell it was a Saturday. It was packed wall to wall. Tiffany texted me letting me know they were already there and had a table by the restrooms. Once I could weave my way through the groups of hungry loud people waiting to be served I found my way to the table I saw not only my girls and Nick, but Roderick, Robert, and none other than mister Q himself. I honestly didn't give two fucks because I was on cloud nine. I sat next to Keisha and eyed her, and she instantly caught on and shrugged pretty much letting me know she didn't know that Q was coming either. I looked over at Tiffany, and she mouthed "sorry" to me.

"Anyways please tell us why the sudden change of heart because just three hours ago you couldn't fuck with us anymore until after graduation." Keisha smart mouth ass said. Looking around the table I saw all eyes on me. Keisha was tapping her fingers on the table as if I was taking forever to speak, but everyone else was just looking.

"Well boo if you must know I got accepted into Wash U! We had to celebrate, but I didn't feel like hitting the club so I felt this was a better spot." Everyone at the table congratulated me. Before I got up, and went to the bar to talk to Robin, and grab me two shots before heading back with the rest of the group. It seemed as if none of us were really hungry which was odd because before I read the acceptance letter I was starving, but now nothing could bother me.

We ordered a large tray of wings and fries, and while we waited for our food and drinks to come we talked about our plans for school, and moving after graduation. Nick and Q kept having side conversations that were in code and even though I was over him I was still very curious to know what they were discussing, but I knew I couldn't come right out and ask since I wasn't speaking to him so I tried to ignore it.

I was tipsy, and had to piss bad after being here for over an hour drinking so I excused myself from the table and walked over towards the restrooms. After I used the bathroom I washed my hands and reapplied my lipstick that was now practically gone. On my way out I bumped into someone that was coming out of the Men's room.

"Oh I'm so sorry I wasn't paying attention." I said as I

looked up into Q's eyes. He had a weird look in his eyes as if he wanted to say something, but he didn't. Before I could push myself back he had his mouth pressed against mine, and was pushing me into the women's room. As bad as I wanted to stop him I couldn't. The way his warm lips felt on me had be ready to throw him my V-card.

His touch was mesmerizing, and I wanted to feel his hands all over my body at this very moment. Every time I opened my eyes and looked at him chills went down my spine. As bad as I wanted more with this man I just couldn't bring myself to be a homewrecker.

He pinned me onto the wall and continued to kiss me passionately. He pulled my straps down on my romper, and attacked my breasts. The chills that I was just feeling had turned into electric shock waves that sent tingles down my spine. The feeling was so good, and for the first time since we had been here I forgot that I was even mad at him.

"Damn Sparkle I want to taste you so bad. Can I taste you baby?" Instead of giving him an answer the only sounds that came out of my mouth was moans. He must have took that as a green light to continue because his kisses started landing everywhere except my lips. He kept licking and sucking all over my breasts until a woman walked into the restroom. The expression on her face was priceless. The old white woman face went from a pale white to a bright red. By the look on her face she wasn't used to seeing people making out in public restrooms. She turned her head as she went into a stall, and we fixed our clothes and left back out to join everyone else.

The rest of the time at Applebee's was awkward. Q kept staring at me, and I tried my hardest to avoid eye contact with him at all cost. I knew I wanted him, but I also knew I couldn't be with him if he was really in a relationship with Brittany.

Two Weeks Later

It had been two weeks since the Applebee's incident, and I have been avoiding Q at all cost. He had popped up at my school a few times, but I would either act like I was running late for class, or I would just hide from him. My conscience wasn't allowing me to give in to him. He had even called several times, and texted me asking if he could meet up with me to talk, but I didn't have time for the baby mama drama so I chose to just reject his offers. He had been blowing my phone up today, but I ignored him. I would be lying if I said I didn't think of him all day every day, but I had to get him out of my mind cause he was no good for me.

Today was the biggest day of my life. In just a few hours me and my bitches will be walking across the stage, and starting our new journey as women. My mom made several appointments for us to look at some apartments closer to the university for after graduation. It was fine by me cause I was getting tired of sneaking in the house after turning up all night.

After graduation me, Tiff, and Keisha took off our caps, and gowns and proceeded to have our own mini photo shoot right there in the parking lot. I had on a plum bodycon dress, some all black red bottoms, and my hair had a loose curl pattern. Tiffany wore a red pencil skirt with a white lace crop top. On her feet, she had on a pair of Michael Kors pumps, and she was still rocking her pixie cut. Keisha had on a bad ass pants suit with just a lace bra under the jacket, and a pair of black Chanel heels.

"How many pictures do y'all plan on taking? We need to be leaving if we are going to make it to these appointments Spark." My mom could be so impatient sometimes. She kept saying she couldn't wait for me to move out of her house, but lowkey I knew she wanted me to stay.

Since we decided to go apartment shopping she has thrown out little hints that she didn't want me to leave. Like yesterday she came in my room telling me I didn't need to rush the process of moving because I had my whole life to be grown. The week before that I caught her sitting in my room crying holding a picture frame of me and her.

"A'ight ma dang. Bye y'all! I'll see y'all later at the dinner." I hopped in the car with my mom, and we were on our way. As she drove she kept crying, and saying how proud she is of me. She was always dramatic so I wasn't really paying her any attention. I was going through all the pictures we just took and posting them to IG. I uploaded three pictures of me, and my girls, and one of myself. The one by myself I captioned *Ass phat yeah I know!* No sooner than I pressed upload my page my Instagram page started going crazy. It only took us about ten minutes to get to the apartments so I threw my phone in my bag, and started my apartment tours.

After two hours of shopping around for the perfect apartment

I decided to sign a lease with a luxury apartment complex in the Central West End. Now that I was done doing that I could finally get home, and get ready for tonight's dinner with all our families, and friends. I decided on a leather cat suit with some black booties from Bakers. I guess my mom didn't feel like waiting on me because by the time I finished getting ready she was gone. I grabbed my purse and left the house.

Damn I still had to get gas, and make the twenty-minute drive to the restaurant. I just hope they didn't start without me. I pulled up to the BP gas station on W. Florissant and hopped out. I went in and bought two shots of Hennessy, and paid to fill up my baby.

When I got to the door of the BP I saw my car windshield had been busted out, and my tires flattened. I was beyond pissed. It didn't take me long at all to pay for the gas, and I didn't hear a damn thing. There were people all around the parking lot, but in this crime infested area no one would tell even if they did see what had happened.

In this area you were going against street code by snitching, and if you did you could end up with a bullet to your head so I wasn't surprised that everyone looked away when they saw me. I took my phone off the car charger, and googled tow trucks in the area. I had to wait thirty minutes for it to arrive, and with all the kids yelling and loud music from the surrounding cars I understood exactly why I didn't hear someone messing with my car. When it did I was in complete shock. Q hopped out of the tow truck, and walked up to my car tapping on the window.

"Did you call for a tow truck?" I turned around so that he could see my face, and pushed my door open. Getting out the car and crossing my arms over my chest I let the attitude drip from my voice.

"Yes, I did. So, here's my address and keys. What do I owe you?" I wasn't in the mood for small talk I still needed to figure out who I was going to have pick me up. Calling my mom was out the question.

"Nothing, consider it a graduation present. So who did you piss off?" I couldn't believe he just asked me that. He barely knew me, but I made it very clear to him that I didn't like drama.

"Actually, smart ass I didn't piss off anyone. I don't do drama, and I don't beef with people. I don't know who would do this." I couldn't help eyeing him, and I was liking what I saw. He was wearing a white wife beater, and some gray sweat pants, and his dick print was very much so apparent. I took another quick glance at it before looking back up at his face.

"Well would you like me to take you home, or do you need me to take you somewhere else? You are my last tow for the night so I don't mind." As bad as I wanted to say no I didn't want to call my mom and have her worried, so I jumped in the front of the tow truck. "So, where the fuck you thought you were going with that tight ass shit on?"

While his words were those of distaste his eyes said something different, and that was that he liked what I had on.

"I was headed to the Ameristar before someone thought it would be funny to fuck up my baby. We're having a graduation dinner there, and there's nothing wrong with my outfit at all."

"Cool I was headed there too to meet up with Nick and Roderick since they've been kicking it with your friends. So why have you been avoiding me?" He now had his body turned facing me in the truck waiting for an answer. This was the worst possible time to be having this conversation. I was practically stranded, and my car was vandalized.

"Look Q like I said before I don't do the drama, and I don't mess with dudes that are already in relationships. You seem like you a good dude, but you come with way too much baggage. Not to mention you live with your baby mama." Without saying anything else he turned back forward, and started the truck. I couldn't help but to admire his toned arms as he gripped the steering wheel. Even though he wasn't trying to his muscles flexed with every motion he made.

"If your stubborn as would have let me explain you would have known from the start that she was only staying with me until her apartment got finished being remodeled. I didn't want her hopping from place to place with my daughter so I said she could crash in the guest room at my apartment. Do you mind if I run to the crib and take a quick shower?" Deep down in my soul I didn't believe him, but he sounded like a standup guy by wanting to his daughter, and not see his child or his child's mother out on the street.

"Nope, I'm already running late, and besides Tiffany just texted saying that there's an hour wait on our tables." We sat in the truck quiet the entire time to my mom's house to drop off my car. I was going to have my dad call his car repairman to come pick up my car and take it to his shop. Once he had it unloaded I made sure all my valuables were secured in the house, and I hopped back into the tow truck.

As we pulled up to his apartment I was surprised to see that he lived in the building next to the one I will be moving in on Monday. I decided to keep my mouth closed and keep that part to myself. As we walked in his apartment I noticed that it was decorated very nice, and cozy.

His living room was decorated in a midnight blue, and grey. He had artwork on the wall, and even a small green plant in the corner next to the balcony door. He gave me a quick tour of the rest of the apartment, and I admired the pictures he had of him, and his daughter on the wall along the hall.

When the quick tour was over he told me to make myself at home while he took his shower. I decided to stay in his room because I didn't want to take the chance of running into Brittany. The chick was so childish, and really needed to grow up. I grabbed the remote, and turned it to Love and Hip Hop Atlanta. I still couldn't believe that MiMi was dating a woman. I didn't even realize that I had dozed off until I felt Q rubbing the side of my face.

"How long have I been sleep?" I said sitting up in his bed. I couldn't help but notice his dick print as he sat next to me with nothing on, but a towel.

"Not long at all." He reached over and placed both of his hands on both sides of my face, and leaned in for a kiss. I leaned in too, and allowed his tongue to dance around my mouth. I swear my body felt so electrified as he kissed all over my mouth and neck. He unzipped the top of my cat suit, and began to play with my now hardened nipples. He pushed me down gently and slowly started taking my clothes off me.

Once I was in nothing, but my panties and bra he just looked over my body like I was the last supper. I was so turned on just from kissing him I wanted to go the next step, but feared that I was getting myself into something I couldn't get out of. I wanted to stop him because deep down my didn't know if I was ready to partake in what was soon to happen.

"Damn ma you sexy as fuck." Q whispered as he kissed all over my stomach, and down to my thighs. When he started pulling on my panties that's when I stopped him. My heart was pounding a million miles a minute as he made my body feel like it had never felt before.

"Wait Q. what are we doing?" I was nervous, and even though I wanted this it just didn't set well with me knowing that Brittany could walk in on us whenever she wanted.

"Shid I'm trying to make you feel good ma. Just lay back and let me take care of you." As he laid over me in a pushup position I tried to relax as I admired his body.

"No seriously I have never done this before and I'm not trying to just give it to anybody." I didn't want to tell him that because I didn't know how he would feel about me if he knew I was a virgin. Most older dudes wanted a female that was advanced, and here I was a virgin, and didn't know what the hell to do.

"Well it's a good thing I'm not just anybody so relax, and let me take care of you. I promise I won't hurt you." For some reason, I believed him when he said he wouldn't hurt me. So, I laid back down and let him go to work.

Once he had my panties off Q took his time placing soft kisses all over my wetness. He began to taste my wetness with his tongue as I let out a soft moan. My mind was gone as he moved his tongue in a circular motion around my juice box. The only thing I could think about was how good he was making me feel.

"Damn baby that feels so good." I managed to say as I ran my fingers over his head. He began going faster and faster adding pressure as he circled my clit. Before I could say anything else I released all my juices over his mouth and face.

"Mmmmm baby you taste so good." I gave him a shy smile, and we began to kiss again. Out of nowhere I felt a sharp pain between my legs like I have never felt before. Tears began to fall from my face as he thrust in and out of my tight opening. I heard my friends talk about how good sex felt, and how they were addicted to it, but this was nothing I could enjoy. The pain was sharp, and it felt like someone had cut my lady part with a razor.

"Are you okay? Do you want me to stop?" He asked as he kissed my tears. I shook my head no because the pain wouldn't allow any words to come out. After a few minutes of pain it slowly turned into pleasure, and I was now slowly enjoying every stroke. It's crazy how at first it felt like I was going to die, but now it was like I was on an all-time high, and didn't want to come down from it.

"Yesss daddy this dick feels so good." I yelled out as he turned me over and entered me from the back.

"Ahhh damn baby this my pussy now. Do you forgive daddy? "My body started shaking uncontrollably, and I released all of my juices. I could honestly get use to this. I see what the hype was all about.

"Yesss daddy yassss!" The next thing I knew Q was releasing his warm cream inside of me. Before we could even catch our breath crazy ass Brittany was beating on his room door, and yelling.

"Get yourself together I'm about to handle her." He kissed me on the forehead before he grabbed a pair of basketball shorts and walked out of the room. We couldn't even lay together, and figure out what we expected from each other before this Tasmanian devil interrupted our moment.

I got up, and ran to the shower. At this moment what I really wanted to do was soak in a hot bath because my lower half was killing me, but I really needed to hurry up and make it to the Ameristar before my mother got worried.

When I finished with my shower I heard them still going at it. I just shook my head and kept getting dressed. He came back in the room a few minutes later just as I finished putting my booties on.

He looked so good walking around shirtless I wanted to go a second round with him, but my little body needed to recover from the first round.

Then I still had thoughts running through my head about what he thought of me. I barely knew this man, and I had just given him something so precious to me. Hopefully he doesn't think I'm a thot because that would be the furthest thing from the truth.

"Let me hop in the shower real quick, and I will be ready." I sat back on the bed and snapped a few pictures and posted them to the gram. My hair wasn't flawless anymore but I could get away with how it looked since it was bone straight. When I finally looked up Q was walking back out of the bathroom, and into his closet.

He came out fully dressed in all black. His look was sexy as fuck to me, but let simple. He was wearing a pair of black jeans, a black polo, and some all black huarache. He looked over at me, and gave me a wink.

"Are you feeling okay babe? "I gave him a small smile, but since he wanted to know I was going to let him know exactly how I felt physically and mentally.

"I'm in some pain down there, but I will be okay."

"Aw, do you want me to kiss it for you to make it feel better?" He leaned over me and started planting kisses down my stomach again. Then out of nowhere he began tickling me. I laughed so hard. No one knew that I was very ticklish, but now he knew, and the harder I laughed the more he tickled me.

"No serious please stop Q I'm for real. I need to say something."

Once he stopped, and I could calm down from laughing I got serious so that I could get my concerns off my chest. "The pain down there will be okay, but I don't want you to think I'm easy, and will have sex with anyone. I'm not a hoe. I don't know what made me have sex with you." It made me so nervous to say what I said, but I wanted to get it off my chest so that he wouldn't think I was just a jump-off.

"Sparkle I don't look at you as a hoe. It's something about you that draws me to you, and even though I don't know what it is exactly I know this was supposed to happen. I told you when we first met you were going to be my wife, and I meant that. The only thing I ask is that you trust me when I tell you something because I want to see where we can go, but with you always running from a nigga you making it hard." Hearing that he didn't think I was a hoe made me feel at ease. I was so thankful that I decided to have that conversation with him because if I would have left his house without this having this conversation I would have been avoiding him again in fear that he thought I was a hoe.

On our way out of his apartment I saw Brittany sitting on the couch with the prettiest little girl I have ever seen in her lap. Whatever Q had said to Brittany must have scared the shit out of her because I was expecting her to see me, and act a damn fool, or maybe she just didn't want to act a fool in front of her daughter.

Whatever the reason was though I was relieved because I didn't feel like fighting. I noticed that Brittany was crying, but hell she brought that on herself. Q walked over to his daughter and gave her a kiss on the cheek and we walked out and headed to our destination.

Chapter 3: Q

When we finally made it to the Ameristar we were well over thirty minutes late. As we walked into the private party area if on cue all eyes were on us. Sparkle walked around the long table kissing everyone, while I just took my seat next to Nick. Sparkle came and sat next to me since that was the only seat left.

We ordered drinks, and joined in on the small talk being held around us. I couldn't help but stare at how beautiful Sparkle was to me. She looked too good laughing, and cracking jokes with her mom. I just only hoped she didn't go M.I.A on a nigga again.

"So Sparkle did you find an apartment that you like?" Her friend Keisha asked her as they chatted. It was pretty dope to see how close she was with her friends. It kind of reminded me of the bond I had with Nick and my brothers.

"Girl yes, and I love it. It's located Lindell, and they're called The York House. I move in Monday so I have a lot of things to get ready before then." Sparkled stated matter of factly. My head spun around so quick to make sure I was hearing her correctly. She looked at me and gave me a guilty smile. I leaned over and whispered in her ear.

"So when did you plan on telling me you were moving into my building?" She looked at me as if I said something funny. "I'm not moving into your building. I'm moving in the one next to yours." Clearly, she didn't know what she was talking about because there was only one set of York House apartments, and that was my building. I decided to let her believe that, but she was in for a shock of her life.

"So Sparkle who is your friend, and where did you two meet?" Her mom asked seriously. "Yes please do tell." Tiffany chimed in all too amused.

"His name is Q, and we met at Chris's party a few weeks ago." Sparkle looked annoyed by her mom's questioning. I didn't know if I should be worried, but I guess I was about to find out.

"So Q is that your government name, or your street name? What do you do for a living to have all of those shiny jewels on?" Sparkle's mom asked. Sparkle put her head down, clearly she was embarrassed by her mother's antics, but this wasn't anything new to me because I went through the same thing with Brittany's mom.

"Actually, my real name is Quentin, but my mom has called me Q since I was younger so it kind of stuck with me. I am the owner of a towing company, and that's how I'm afforded the luxuries I have." I was really trying to play nice, but if she popped slick all bets would be off. I see where Sparkle get her looks from though. If I didn't know the singer Aaliyah was dead I swear I would have thought Sparkle's mom was her. She had Aaliyah's body frame, skin complexion, and long dark hair just like her.

"Well it's nice to meet you. Although I have to ask what are your intentions with my daughter?" At this point I didn't want to say well I just got in them guts, and I think she's sexy as fuck. So I went with the best answer I could think of.

"We're seeing where things go, but I am really feeling her." Her mom didn't say anything after that, she just nodded her head, and started talking to the lady sitting on the other side of her. I didn't know if that was a good thing or a bad one, but I didn't give a fuck either. I had made up my mind that I wanted to be with Sparkle and I wasn't going to let anyone get in between us again.

"Aye bruh we need to chop it up asap about the yard." Roderick said. That was code for we needed to talk about the shipment of guns we had coming in next week. That's right I sell guns on the streets as my real occupation, and use the towing company to clean up my dirty money.

"Cool let's step outside real quick." I just pray that everything was on schedule. The last thing I needed was for some shit to go wrong right now.

We got up from the table and headed out of the restaurant. As we walked through the casino Roderick began to talk. "So everything is all set for next week, however that nigga Tim has been acting real suspect lately, and his numbers were off last week. I think we need to pay that nigga a visit since he seems to can't get shit right." Roderick was only eighteen and had a full ride scholarship to play ball at SLU.

He wasn't into school, but his life revolved around basketball so he made sure his grades were straight. He was my enforcer on the streets though. Him and Robert was quick to put lead in any nigga that felt the need to cross us, or late paying up.

"We can handle that nigga tomorrow just have Rob keep eyes on that fool until we holla at him. What's good with you and ol girl Keisha?" Hopefully this fool didn't fuck things up because I didn't want anything to interfere with what I was trying to build with Sparkle, and females always sided with their friends.

"Shit you know me big bro I'm trying to fuck, but her last nigga got her head all fucked up, so we just been coolin' it. What's up with her homegirl though? I saw yo ass cheesin' real hard when y'all walked in here." I didn't want to sound soft or no shit like that cause lil mama had me open.

"Shit the same as you and her friend. We just kickin' it. I been trying to fuck with her heavy, but she not feeling the whole Brittany situation. Speaking of which we were fucking earlier, and Brittany came home with Mya, and the bitch started banging on my door talking about I'm disrespecting her, and I shouldn't have Sparkle in the crib. I damn near choked her dumb ass out. She in my shit, and thinks I'm supposed to not have bitches over cause she's there."

"Bruh you better be careful Brittany's ass is crazy. You remember the last chick you was messing with she tried to hit with her car." Roderick ass was laughing hard as hell, but he was telling the truth. Brittany didn't care if people thought she was crazy she wasn't about to see me happy with anybody but her.

"I know, I'm ready to make that bitch find a new spot to stay, but then I won't see Mya every day, but check this shit out. Sparkle is moving in my building." Roderick looked at me as if I had two heads.

"Wait so she trying to be up under you like that already ready? Nigga that's a fatal attraction." I couldn't help but to laugh cause he was dead ass serious.

"Nah bruh she didn't know I stayed there until just a few hours ago, and by the sound of things she been picked out the apartment. I just hope I can keep her and Brittany away from each other cause if not I'm going to have a shit load of trouble on my hands."

Once we got back to the table everyone was wrapping up to leave. I grabbed the bill folder off the table and placed my black card in it.

"Is everything okay? You were gone for a while." Sparkle asked once I sat back down. I could get use to her sexy ass checking on me. She had the cutest little wrinkle in her forehead as she asked.

"Yeah I'm good baby we just had to go over some business that's all. So are you coming back to my spot so we can get to know each other better, or am I taking you home?" While I wanted to be inside of her again I did really want to get to know her more. She just didn't realize she had my head gone.

"That depends, will crazy lady be there ready for war?" I chuckled because she thought she was funny. The looked she had plastered on her face was a playful one, but I knew the question was serious. I need to find a way to get rid of Brittany because I really do see a future with Sparkle, and the way I see it Brittany would try to fuck it up like the last chick.

"Nah you're in good hands. I got you baby.

"Well in that case let's go." She kissed her family and friends bye, but before could we headed out her mom stopped her.

"Sparkle where do you think you're going? All your family and friends are here to celebrate your big accomplishment, and you're trying to run off with some nappy head ass boy. I think you need to sit back down, and enjoy the company of your loved ones." I knew from the way her mom looked at me she didn't care for me, but hell I'm not trying to fuck her. I'm trying to get to know her daughter.

"Ma chill out. I'm just going to hangout for a while, and besides dinner is over. I can see everybody anytime." Sparkle body language was tense, and she looked embarrassed by the way her mom was acting, and truthfully I couldn't blame her. She was technically grown now.

She just finished high school, made her own money, and was moving into her own spot so there was no reason in my eyes for her mom to be tripping. The lady sitting next to Sparkle's mom grabbed her mom's arm, and said something in her ear. I guess she was telling her to let her leave, but I wasn't too sure.

"I don't give a fuck what you are going to do. You better have your ass home at a decent hour, or don't come home at all. I'm not playing with your ass Sparkle, and you better not touch my daughter or I will have buried under the jail." I raised my hands in a surrender. I planned on touching Sparkle, but I wasn't about to let her know that. She was like a lion protecting her cubs.

"I promise I will have her home at a decent hour, and she is in good hands ma'am. I felt like I was being interrogated at first, but now it just felt like her mom wanted me as far away from Sparkle as possible. That was not going to happen though because if I could have things my way Sparkle was going to be mine for the long run. Once we got back to my apartment it was after ten. Sparkle took her heels off and sat Indian style on the couch. I walked to the kitchen to grab me a bottle of Hennessy, and to get her whatever she wanted.

"Do you want anything to drink? I have water, juice, and Henny." I was hoping she wanted some Henny because I wanted her to be loose, and not so guarded.

"A bottle of water if you have one please." I came back in the living room and sat on the opposite end of the couch.

"So tell me all about Sparkle." I handed her the bottle of water as she began to talk. She told me how her dad left her mom three years ago because her mom was always bitching about the smallest things, and her dad couldn't take it anymore. She said she wanted to live with him, but because he was never at home because of work both of her parents thought it would be best if she stayed with her mom.

She told me that she had three older brothers that were out of the house as well. Just like her they moved as soon as they graduated high school. It didn't take a rocket scientist to figure out that Sparkle's mom was high strung, and running everybody away from her. Also, how her and her brothers were close, but they started traveling more doing work with their dad.

She went on to tell me that she makes her money by hosting parties, and posting pictures on Instagram for sponsors. I thought it was dope how she found a hustle out of taking pictures of herself. Most hoes out here were posting half naked pictures on social media for free, and she used it for a come up.

"Now that you know about my boring life Quentin tell me about yourself." That was another plus in my eyes for Sparkle. Most of the females I came across could care less about what I was doing with myself. The only thing they cared about was what I could do for them. Case in point Brittany. I knew she didn't love me. With Brittany, she just wanted the money, and she felt if I had another female she would lose those benefits.

"Well my mom was a single mother of six bad ass kids, four boys and two girls. I'm the second oldest child. My older brother was gunned down when I was younger. Ever since he was killed my mom has been overprotective of all her kids, but just recently she moved out of state to take a new job." She asked about Mya, and I told her that Brittany, and I were high school sweethearts, but we broke up over a year ago, after I found out she was cheating. She didn't try to pry information out of me that I wasn't willing to offer, or that I just didn't want to talk about. We laughed, and talked about random shit for hours, and it made me like her even more. She was so down to earth, and wasn't just a pretty face with a nice body. She wanted more out of life.

I guess we talked until we fell asleep right there on the couch because we woke up to pots being slammed down in the kitchen.

"Oh, I'm sorry did I wake you?" Brittany asked with a smirk on her face. Honestly, I didn't even know Brittany was even here. I guess I was so wrapped up in getting to know Sparkle I just figured Brittany, and Mya were at her mom's house. I grabbed Sparkle's hand and led her to my room.

"Do you mind if I take a quick shower?" Sparkle asked just as we made it to the room. I shook my head to let her know I didn't mind and before I could even close the door I heard Mya crying so I went in the guest room and picked her up. My baby girl was the highlight of my world.

Her smile was what I needed when I was having a rough day, and her coos and laughs warmed my heart on the coldest days. My baby girl was my world. When I got back to my room I heard water running in the bathroom so I figured that Sparkle was already taking a shower. I laid Mya down on my bed, and grabbed Sparkle a wife beater, and a pair of my basketball shorts to put on. I sat them in the bathroom, and went back to tend to Mya.

She came out of the bathroom a few minutes later looking so good. She had her hair pulled up into a ponytail, and my basketball shorts were swallowing her small body. She hopped on my bed and sat next to me while I played with Mya in my lap.

"She is so adorable! Can I hold her?" I was surprised she wanted to hold her, and I wasn't too sure about her being around my baby but I let her anyway. I figured if she was going to be a part of my life she had to at least like my child. What surprised me more was that Brittany didn't come in here acting crazy. She was overprotective of Mya, and come to think of it her behavior was odd. Brittany never missed a chance to be petty, or to keep up drama so for her to not be acting a damn fool right now was a shock.

"So what's your plan for today ma?" I wanted to chill with her if possible, but I knew she had to get home. "Do you think your mom is going to trip for you staying out all night? "I forgot that I promised to have her home at a decent hour, but fuck we fell asleep so I couldn't control that.

"Naw she won't even be there because she has to work. I might have to hear her mouth later, but it's nothing I'm not use to. However, I have to rent a car, and then I want to go to Ikea to get so things for the apartment." I was hoping she didn't have plans because I didn't want her to leave, but it looked as if luck wasn't on my side.

"Let's go out to breakfast, and then I can take you home." I got dressed, took Mya in the room with Brittany, and we headed out.

On the drive to drop Sparkle off we made small talk, and before she got out of the car we promised to link up later. I kissed her as she got out of the car, and made sure she made it in the house safe before I pulled off. After I dropped Sparkle off I sent Nick, Tim and Roderick a text letting them know to me meet me at The Yard in thirty minutes.

The yard was an old abandoned junkyard that housed broke down cars. This is where we handled all business that required getting our hands dirty. After making a few calls to some local hustlers in the JVL projects I found out that Tim was indeed taking money from me.

Selling guns was like my second child. I took this business very serious. Everyone knew that I didn't pay when it came to what I did. A perk to selling weapons was that everyone knew who I was, and very few people tried to cross me because I didn't mind making an example out of those who did.

It had been a minute since I let my glock ring, but since niggas didn't have respect I was about to show him what God looked like. It took all of them a little over an hour to get here, but once they made it to the back I got straight down to business. Fuck the pleasantries when dealing with my money. When it came to money fuck a friend when you had Benjamins.

"So Tim I see that yo numbers came up short last week. Was there something wrong with the package you had?" I was trying my hardest not to dead this nigga right now. I wanted to hear what he had to say first. It didn't matter either way because he was on borrowed time, but maybe he could produce my money before I offed his ass.

"Nah boss everything was straight. I thought the numbers were right." Tim sounded so fucking dumb. This nigga is supposed to count the money before handing over any gun. So either he wasn't counting the money or he was stealing, and either way I didn't have room on my team for a nigga to be fucking up.

"What the fuck you mean you thought?! Bitch ass nigga do I pay you to think? You have just under a minute to come up with my hundred stacks." I told him as calmly as I could. I pulled a Kush blunt from behind my ear and lit it as I counted down.

"But boss I can't com…" Before he had a chance to say anything else I let off one shot to his dome. I wasn't successful in my line of work by letting people steal from me, and not doing shit about it. I made a name for myself by being ruthless, and that wasn't about to change for anyone.

"Call the cleanup crew, and tell them to feed that nigga to the piranhas. No face, no case." I handed Roderick the blunt, and walked to my car. I sat there for a minute stuck in my thoughts before pulling off. I still couldn't believe that nigga tried to steal from me. Turning my radio on I instantly felt better. *Hot 104.1* was playing Drake's *Back to Back*, and that was my joint. I wanted to hit Sparkle up, but didn't want *to* seem thirsty so I deaded that idea, and went to my crib.

To my relief, Brittany old nagging, bald headed ass wasn't home. I still have been messing with her on and off since I met Sparkle, but it wasn't on no serious shit. We both had that understanding, and so far, Brittany hasn't said shit. Today I planned on ending our sexual relationship so that I could make it exclusive with Sparkle.

I hopped in the shower, and when I got out I went straight to the kitchen to cook me something to eat. I sat on the couch with a big cup of red kool aid, and started eating. These pizza rolls were on point, but what I really needed was a home cooked meal. Once I finished eating I hit baby girl's line.

"Hello!" I started smiling once I heard her voice come through my line. She was starting to have a positive effect on me. It seemed like since I met her I couldn't go a day without seeing her, and the days I did that shit had me tripping.

"What's good baby? Where you at?" I wanted to see her bad. It was something about her that had my head gone. Maybe it was her ability to take my mind off all the bullshit going on around me, or maybe it was just her cool laid back personality. Whatever it was though I wanted more of it.

"Heading home. Why are you coming to see me?" Damn I guess she was missing me too. Hopefully her mom was still at work when I got there cause I didn't have time to hear her mouth.

"Yeah give me a few minutes, and I'll be on my way."

"Cool just text me when you're headed my way." She sounded excited as she made her last statement, but hell I was too so that made two of us. I only had on a pair of basketball shorts, and a wife beater but fuck it I needed a quick release and Sparkle was just the person to get me right. I went to the safe in my room, and took my burner out.

She lived in the Ville and I was not trying to get caught slipping over there. I grew up in the JVL so I wasn't scared of them Ville niggas at all. JeffVanderLou projects or JVL for short was one of the worst areas to live in. The crime rate was always at an all-time high. The homes were rundown, and everyday someone was fighting, or shooting.

For those of us that grew up over there it was just another day in the hood, but for those visiting you would think you had walked into the middle of a war. Even though I wasn't afraid of the niggas from the Ville I still wasn't about to go over there without my shit. I shot her a quick text letting her know I was on my way, and headed out.

I couldn't help but smile as she opened the door for me in nothing but a t shirt. She hopped up on me wrapping her legs around my waist.

"You smell good." I said as I grabbed her ass noticing she didn't have on any panties. She got down, and led me to her room. For her to live in the Ville her moms had the house looking like something out of that chick magazine *Good Housekeeping*. When we got to her room she closed the door behind us, and like magic our bodies became one. Baby girl was kissing all over a nigga.

"You miss a nigga huh?" She gave me a devilish grin as shook her head. She pushed me on the bed, and took my clothes off me as she stood in front of me. She stood in between my legs, and slowly pulled the t shirt over her head. I used my finger to motion for her to come to me.

Once she straddled me my manhood instantly rose to the occasion. I lifted her just enough to place her on top of my pole, and helped her adjust to the length. At first, she was so stiff and afraid to move. I guess she was still getting use to this whole sex thing, but I had a trick for that ass. I started grinding my hips at a faster pace, and after a few minutes she started moaning. She placed her hands on my chest and took over.

"Damn ma this pussy so wet, and tight." When I opened my eyes, and looked at her, she was in a world of her own. She had her head thrown back, and the sounds that were coming from her gave me chills.

At that moment I knew she would be the one. Just when I was about to get my nut off her door opened and there stood her mom.

"What the fuck are you doing?! Wrap this shit up now, and get his ass out my damn house!"

Chapter 4: Keisha

"Bitch lies! She caught y'all doing what?" I damn near choked on the soda I was drinking. I couldn't believe what I was hearing.

"You heard me bitch. She caught me riding that dick, and made me put his ass out before either one of us came. She was straight on her hating shit." Sparkle couldn't help but laugh as she told me what happened. What had me surprised was my bitch gave her V card to a nigga she has only known for a month or so. I chuckled thinking about how she's a big girl now.

"So what are we doing today?" I had to ask because Sparkle didn't just pop up unless she wanted something. "Well bestie I wanted you to come with me to do the walk through for my apartment since my mom not talking to me at all. I also have to pick my car from the shop. Afterwards I was thinking we go to Fairground park, and turn the fuck up." This bitch knew that talking about turning up was going to win me over.

"Bet, I'm down." My plan this summer was simple, get fucked up, party, and get this money. Fuck a nigga. I was with Jason's ass for two years, and not only did he cheat on me every chance he got he had the audacity to fuck my best friend since first grade. I was kicking it with Q's brother Roderick but honestly I wasn't trying to go there with his ass either. He was cool, but the nigga thought I was stupid I knew he wanted me to drop them draws.

"Let's head the fuck out cause it's already after one, and you know the park about to be doing numbers. We can take my car."

We pulled up to her new apartment, and went in. The outside of the apartments were beautiful so I knew the inside was going to be nice. The old moth balls smelling bitch in the leasing office greeted us, and escorted us to the elevators. As we walked to the elevators I notices the crystal chandeliers and beautiful decorations that lined the walls of the entryway. When she pressed three I just knew this bitch Sparkle was going to die.

"Damn bitch is you okay? You know what don't answer that." The last time I asked that question Tiffany retarded ass was faking. I wasn't about to set myself up for failure a second time. My friends have always been dramatic and I was used to it.

"Yeah I'm good." Once we got off the elevators granny told us the apartment was 36F the last door to the right. She handed Sparkle the keys, and got back on the elevator. This floor had the exact same chandeliers, and wall decorations as the main level. When Sparkle opened the door my mouth damn near hit the floor.

"This is so pretty girl!" The living room had floor to ceiling windows, the kitchen was so bright, and had all brand-new state of the art appliances. Her bathroom looked like something out of a movie. It had a walk-in shower, double vanity, and marble countertops. We walked around and made sure everything was on point. Sparkle walked in the kitchen, and hopped on the counter to sit down.

"Bitch why is this the exact same building Q lives in. Oh but it gets worse. This is the exact same floor too." I wanted to ask her if she was joking, but the expression on her face was letting me know she was dead ass.

"So what are you going to do? If I were you I would ask for a new apartment on a different floor. This is just too close for comfort." I was blown away by what she had just said. Everyone knew Sparkle hated drama, and living on the same floor of her new boo and his baby mama was a recipe for disaster at least in my eyes. That chick Brittany just didn't rub me the right way. I mean what female wants to live with her baby daddy if they aren't together. Not only that, but she looks sneaky as hell.

"I'm not going to ask to be moved. When I want to see, him I will, and when I don't I won't. As a matter of fact I'm not going to even tell him which apartment is mine." She sounded so sure of her idea, but let's be real he was bound to see her sooner or later.

"This is some crazy shit let's bounce." I was ready to go turn up. After she got her keys I dropped her off at her car, and we made our way to Fairground. Once we made it to the park we found two spots in the grass and parked. That was a shock to have found parking spots because Fairground park was always super packed, and if you weren't there before it got crowded you had to park far away and walk over to the park. I was praying like hell that Jason had to work because if he saw my car I knew he was going to show his ass. Since the party I haven't spoken to him. He kept calling so I blocked his ass.

My car stood out so hopefully baby Jesus was on my side today and kept that crazy nigga away from me. I had a 2014 baby

pink Camaro with pink rims, and my bitch stood out wherever I
went. I popped my trunk and grabbed a bottle of 1800 out with two
plastic cups. Sparkle walked over and grabbed a cup just as I
finished filling them up. We looked too cute today. We both had on
a pair of denim shorts that had our ass cheeks playing peekaboo. I
had on a black crop top with some black and white J's. Sparkle had
on white crop top with some all-white low top forces.

"Have you talked to Tiffany today?" Sparkle asked as she
took a sip from her cup.

"Yeah she already here. She said she's right across from
Beaumont." I reached in my car and turned up the radio.

Ass fat, yeah I know,

You just got cash?

blow sum mo' blow sum mo

Rae Sremmurd *Throw Sum Mo* was on, and any song talking
about a fat ass was my song. We were bouncing and shaking our
asses to the lyrics.

"Aye that's my best friend!" I yelled as I watched my boo

Spark twerk sumn'. I went in my purse and grabbed some money out.

Bad Bitches on the flo

It's raining hundreds

Throw sum mo, throw sum mo

Throw sum mo

On cue with the lyrics I made it rain on my bitch. Money was no problem for us. We were young, getting paper faster than we could count it, and living life. I didn't have a man so I was trying my hardest to live life to the fullest, even if it meant making it rain in the park.

"This what the fuck I'm talking about." Some sexy ass nigga said as he got behind Sparkle. When the song was over dude walked away, but not before telling us he would be back.

"Smile for the camera bitch." Sparkle said as she leaned close to me for a picture. She immediately posted it to Instagram, and captioned it *Best friend goals #Slimthick #Ass4days*.

"Girl did you see ol boy that I was dancing with? He was sexy as fuck, and I know he paid I saw that Hermes belt from a mile away." Just like Sparkle to notice a damn belt. I loved my best friend to death, but she was a certified shopaholic. She could spot a fake item from a mile away.

"Yeah I saw him. The real question is do he have a friend?" I was so serious. With me being single I was going to take to as many niggas as I could, and maybe I would run into the right one.

"Yep that's where he went. Here they come now." Sparkle walked up to the dude she was dancing with earlier, and I watched as his friend walked up to me. We were chopping it up when I noticed Nick out the side of my eye. He just walked pass, and didn't say shit so I figured he was looking for Tiffany. I looked over and saw ol boy rubbing all over Sparkle's ass.

I knew that bitch was lit cause she would have never let a random ass nigga be in her personal space like that. No sooner than I turned back around I was getting snatched up by Roderick. Just when I thought I had to worry about Jason's ass. I should have thought about this fool.

"What's good ma? So you out here half naked, and got niggas in yo face and shit." Roderick was all in my face questioning me like we were a couple.

"Man let me go." I told him as I yanked my arm away from

him. "Nigga we are not a couple so don't even try to play me in front of all these people." He had me thirty-eight hot trying to check me like I'm some lil ass girl.

"Cool you got that." He said as he walked away. I could give two fucks though cause I was trying to have fun, and live life. Like I said before fuck a nigga. I turned to look for Sparkle, and I noticed Q had her hemmed up by her shirt on her car. I walked over there cause I was not opposed to fighting a nigga today.

"So you entertaining other niggas now huh? Out here with this lil ass shit on shaking yo ass!" Q yelled as he got closer to Sparkle's face.

"Damn Q you mad huh?" I laughed. I knew I was being petty, but I didn't give a fuck. We weren't doing anything wrong, and from what I understood they weren't official yet either.

"Yeah Q you a little too mad aren't you?" I turned my head to see who was in my damn ear. Instantly I shook my head. This bitch Brittany was like a fly on shit. She just appeared out of nowhere. Wherever Q was you saw this hoe.

"Why are you worried about that ugly ass bitch anyway when you got me?" I couldn't believe this bitch, but she kept talking. "You

all in her face, but I was just sucking your dick this morning."
Brittany kept going on and on.

"Girl fuck these hoes let's go." Now I knew that voice from anywhere. I looked just over Brittany's shoulder, and there stood Ebony. These hoes here just didn't know when to bow down. Before I knew it Sparkle was beating the shit out of Brittany. She had Brittany's head in between the front wheel of her car, and a tree. As soon as Ebony tried to break it up I was on her ass. I kicked that bitch as hard ass I could in her back, making her fall into her friend. I just kept stomping her. It took a minute, but Nick, and Q managed to break up the fights.

"I swear niggas ain't shit! You had me riding the dick, her sucking it, and then turn around and complain cause I'm talking to another nigga!" My bitch was hot, but I felt what she was saying.

"Call me later boo." Sparkle said as she hopped in her car, and pulled off. By the time Tiffany got through the thick ass crowd that had formed I was sitting on the hood of my car smoking that gas. I knew Sparkle was pissed because she hates drama, but not me, or Tiff we lived for that shit.

"Please tell me y'all wasn't the ones fighting." She said

sounding disappointed. She always wanted to be in the middle of our beefs. It never failed if we had a fight, and she wasn't present she would be mad.

"Okay I won't then, but if you must know none of this shit wouldn't have popped off if your boyfriend would have kept his mouth closed." I take it by looking at her face she didn't know Nick had told Q, and Roderick what he saw, so I decided to fill her in.

When I finished my blunt I hopped off my car, gave my bestie a hug, and left. I had a headache, and needed to check on Spark.

Chapter 5: Sparkle

Q had me so fucked up if he thought he could play me like I'm just some jumpoff. It's cool though cause if that's how he wanted to play it I was cool with it. Since I lived in the same building with him I made sure to be dressed for the Gods whenever I stepped out my apartment; even to take out my trash.

Him or his bitch wouldn't get the satisfaction of seeing me looking a mess. It's been over a week since I laid hands on Brittany, and I still felt slighted about what she said.

When I left the park that day I went straight to Walgreens and bought a Plan B. Today was going to be a good day for me. It was the annual Summer skate party at Skate King, and the owner paid the TDPs a pretty penny for us to host the event this year.

Tiffany had texted me earlier saying to pick her up, so that's where I was headed now. I turned all the lights out in my apartment, and headed to the door. As I was locking up I felt a pair of eyes on me. I looked up, and there Q was watching me. I didn't want him to know I stayed on his floor at all, and here I was standing in front of him. I tried to brush past him, but he caught my arm. I knew I would see him around, but I didn't expect for him to see me coming out of my apartment.

"What damn?" I asked with as much attitude in my voice as possible. If he thought he was going to have both of us he was sadly mistaking Sparkle plays second to no one.

"I understand you're mad, but just hear me out. "He actually had the nerves to be looking sad. Here it is his baby mama that lives with him had just admitted they are still messing around, and he has the nerves to look sad. Brittany is a dumb bitch for sitting around allowing the man she is involved with to have sex with other people while she sits back and cry about it. Instead of her hating the females she needs to move the fuck on, and stop letting Q use her as a doormat.

"Oh I'm not mad. In order for me to be mad I have to give a fuck, and I don't so we're good." I was hella mad, but I wasn't going to tell him that. No man walking this earth would get the satisfaction of thinking they've gotten under my skin.

"Well I'll let you go then. By the way you look nice." Q said in a low tone. Lowkey though he looked good too. He was sporting a red and white STL fitted cap. His shirt was a white Ralph Lauren

shirt with the red logo, and he was wearing some dark denim jeans.

On his feet he had on a pair of red and white Jordan twelves.

"Thanks." I walked off and before I could step on the

elevator he was calling my name. I turned around to face him.

"I miss you for real." I had to chuckle at that cause he seriously had

me messed up. As bad as I missed his ass I refused to even say those

words back. So I said what was on my mind, and not my punk ass

heart.

"Yeah what the fuck ever nigga," and hopped on the elevator.

Pulling up at Tiffany's house was like pulling up at a 24-hour

club. It stayed popping in Walnut Park especially her block. Walnut

Park was a neighborhood on the North side of Saint Louis. Like

most of the other neighborhoods in the city of Saint Louis Walnut

Park was filled with drugs, crime, and drama. Even the police feared

to go in that area, and when they did they made it as quick as

possible.

Tiffany lived on Alcott with her mom, grandma, and younger

brother. I loved coming over here because it was always something

going on, and today was no different. As soon as I got out of my car

I walked to the corner where I saw all the commotion. Some lady had a brick in one hand, and a butcher's knife in the other. She threw the brick through the back, of an old-school car, and then started running down the street towards the mail truck. I heard a man yelling, and noticed he was running from her. He jumped on the back of the mail truck and held on for dear life. I was laughing so hard I had tears coming down my face.

"Hey boo!" I was laughing so hard I didn't even see Tiffany and Nick approach me. "What's poppin bestie?" I loved Tiffany she was ghetto as hell, but I loved her like a sister.

"Hey Nick!" I gave him a hug, and asked Tiffany was she ready to go. I didn't want to see Nick or his dumb ass friend.

"Yasss bitch let's get to the money!" She gave Nick a kiss, and we hopped in my car and left. "Girl I'm surprised you gave Nick a hug. I thought you would be mad at him. "I looked at her like she was crazy.

"Shit it's not like he made the nigga get his dick sucked." Tiffany was laughing, but I was dead ass serious. Fuck Q and his bitch. The whole drive Tiffany wanted to talk about Q and Brittany, but I kept changing the topic.

When we got to Skate King I hit the alarm on my car, and we bypassed all the waiting people and entered. The first stop we made was to the office to meet with Mrs. Moore to discuss what was expected for us, and to collect our pay. This was about to be an easy night if we didn't have any problems. I walked to my car, and took my skates out of my trunk. I slammed the trunk closed, and instantly became pissed. Brittany, and her bum squad was walking pass.

Putting my game face on I walked up to them. I thanked them for coming to our event, and walked off. That's right I was being Petty LaBelle, and was enjoying every moment of it.

"No thank you for leaving my man alone. I would have hated to have him tell you to your face." She was really trying me, but it was cool because I always get the last laugh. Going back into the rink I found a spot to sit so that I could put my skates on.

"I thought I wasn't going to see you again after yo dude snatched yo lil fine ass up." I looked up to see Steve standing in front of me. Steve was the dude I met at Fairground park the day all that shit popped off.

"Nah that ain't my man, and I was hoping I saw you here today since we didn't get to exchange numbers that day." He held his hand out for me to grab as I finished lacing up my skates. I grabbed his hand. He led us to the rink, and we started skating together just as T.I song *Got Your Back* came on.

> *When we're high,*
> *When we're low,*
> *Boy I promise I will never let you go,*
> *Said I got I got I got I got your back boy*

Jason was holding my hand as we did laps around the rink. When I saw Q staring at us, I turned around and started skating backwards in front of Jason. Q looked like he wanted to kill me and Steve, but I was soaking it up. Out the corner of my eye I spotted Brittany grilling Q.

I started singing the lyrics to the song to him, and placed his hands on my waist. One thing about me was I could be as petty as the next bitch, and even more petty if pushed to the limit. We skated together for a few more songs before I got thirsty, and needed something to drink.

When we got off the rink I put my number in his phone and we went our separate ways. I skated over to the concession stand were I saw my bitches at.

"You look cute boo! Keisha said as she gave me a hug.

"Thanks boo I try. You don't look too bad yourself." I was rocking a navy blue quilted skater skirt, and a form fitting top. I had my hair half up in a bun, and the other half down, and for accessories were some gold bangles, and some gold bamboo earrings.

"Girl I am having too much fun. Steve is so down to earth, and funny." It felt good to let go, and not have to worry about a bitch running up on you cause you talking to her man.

"Bitch you need to be careful because Nick had to stop Q from pulling your ass off that damn rink." Tiffany stated while looking past me.

"At this point on my life it is all about me, and I could care less about him and his feelings." Every word that was coming out of my mouth was how I really felt. I wanted to be with a person that made me feel special.

"Yeah okay tell that to him." She said smiling while pointing her finger behind me. When I turned around Q was standing there with his jaws tight so I knew he was pissed, but oh well. I smiled at him, grabbed my soda off the counter, and began to skate away. Q snatched me up again by my arm almost making me lose my balance on these skates.

"Damn I see you have a problem with keeping your hands to yourself. What do you want now?" I was getting tired of him trying to treat me like a fucking kid. At the same time though his touch was driving me crazy. I missed feeling him already.

"I see you keep disrespecting me. I know I told your ass to stop entertaining other niggas. Don't get him fucked up Spark." I sat down on the bench next to where I was standing. I took my skates off so that I could go to the restroom. Like the imposing fool he was he was right on my heels, and in my personal space again.

"Can I have some privacy please?" I had to ask him cause it was clear that he wasn't going to give me the space I needed. I went in the restroom, and handled my business. After I washed my hands, and headed out I noticed he wasn't by the door. I saw him across the room talking to Brittany. I quickly went to the locker that had my stuff in it, and grabbed my booties to put back on.

Scanning the venue, I noticed Steve sitting on the bench by

SPARKLE OF HIS EYE

the concession stand texting so I walked over to him and started to sit down, but to my surprise he pulled me on his lap. Keisha and Tiffany walked up and started chopping it up with us. I was really enjoying myself. I pulled out my iPhone 6s plus and snapped a picture of me and Steve. I captioned it *My Mister???*

I grabbed the plastic cup from Keisha's hand and took a sip. I knew that bitch had something strong in it. She pulled a bottle of Cîroc out of her purse and poured me a cup. I shook my head cause she was Oso ghetto.

She handed me my cup and I started downing it instantly. I was trying to get fucked up because I didn't want to deal with Quentin sober. I handed Tiffany my phone and told her to take pictures of me and Jason. I pulled him up so that we could pose for the picture.

After the party started dying down I told my chicas bye, and had Steve walk me to my car. When I got to my car my blood started to boil. Somebody had spray painted HOE all over the sides of my car. It must have been written all over my face that I was ready to explode because Steve rubbed my back, and spoke to me in a calm voice.

"It's cool ma I can take you home if you want." Steve offered. It pissed me off that nobody ever saw anything, or said anything if they did. At this point I was over being well known. The money I made was great, and the offers different companies gave me were like dreams come true, but the constant hate I got from females was too much at times.

"Please I will have it picked up later, and I can pay to fill up your tank." We walked over to his white Range Rover and hopped in. I gave him my address and he typed it into his GPS and we left.

We didn't speak at all as he drove me home. I was trying to figure out exactly who kept messing with my car. This time I had a good idea of who it could be, but I wasn't for sure.

Once we got to my building I asked him if he wanted to come in. Even though it was just before midnight I wasn't tired. He agreed to come up for a second. When we made it to my door I had to dig in my purse and find my keys. I opened the door and let Steve walk in first. I looked down the hall and saw Q watching us so I smiled, winked at him, and walked in.

Walking to the kitchen I grabbed me a bottle of water out of the fridge. I yelled into the living room and asked Steve did he want anything. I grabbed another bottle of water and headed back to the living room. He was walking around looking at the pictures of me, and my friends. We sat down on the couch and I allowed him to find something to watch on TV.

To my surprise he turn turned on *Belly* which was my all-time favorite movie. He laid his head on my lap, and I ran my hands through his dreads.

By the time the movie was over Steve was knocked out. I decided to take a shower, and change into something more comfortable. I grabbed a sheet out of the linen closet and went to place it over Steve. He was sleeping so peaceful I didn't want to wake him.

As I was walking back to my room to go to bed I heard beating on my door. I ran to it so that whoever it was wouldn't wake Steve. When I snatched it open Q stood there pissed off. I was really getting tired of seeing him. I stepped out the door and closed it behind me.

"What do you want at this hour?" I asked him. Crossing my arms over my chest, and tapping my foot to let him know my patience was running thin.

"Stop fucking playing with me! What the fuck that nigga doing in your crib?" This nigga had to be high because I didn't understand how he could be questioning me when he had a whole family down the hall.

"Look Q it's none of your business what he or anyone else is doing at my house. You have a whole family down the hall. Shouldn't you be getting your dick sucked?" I was fuming the one moment I give myself away he had to be a player.

"I didn't come here to argue so go tell that nigga he gotta bounce. Either you do it or I will, but either way he gotta go."

"Look Quentin you don't run shit down here so get the fuck out of my face. You may run shit down the hall, but around this way you ain't running shit." I said before opening my door, and slammed the door in Q's face. When I walked in Steve was folding the sheet I had gave him, and was walking to the door.

"Thanks for letting a nigga chill, but I gotta make some moves." He said placing a kiss on my cheek, and heading to the door. I walked him to the door, and gave him a hug as he exited my apartment, and promised to call him soon. When I finally made it back to my room I flopped across my bed, and as soon as my head hit the pillow I was out.

Chapter 6: Q

I couldn't believe she had slammed the door in my face. I went back to my apartment, and grabbed me a bottle of Remy 1738 off my dry bar. I took it to the head as I sat on my couch mad at the fucking world. I couldn't sit here, and dwell on the situation because we had a shipment coming in a few hours, and I needed to have my head in the game.

I needed to talk to Sparkle though cause if not I wouldn't be able to concentrate on shit. She knew what the fuck she was doing at Skate King wearing that little ass skirt, and messing with that fuck boy. I wanted to beat that nigga's ass, but I knew that would only push her further away. Yeah I let Brittany suck my dick, but what did she expect would happen after her mama bust in on us fucking. I had to release the beast, and Brittany's ratchet ass was at my crib so it only felt right.

The next morning I woke up, hopped in the shower, and got dressed. As I was walking down the hallway I overheard Brittany in her room telling somebody she fucked up Sparkle's car again. I couldn't believe what I was hearing. I pushed the door open, and her dumb ass jumped back dropping her phone, and cracking the screen.

"Who you talking to?" I asked her. One thing I didn't play about was people fucking with those I cared about, and Sparkle was slowly making her way to the top of that list.

"None of your fucking business nigga." She was sitting on her bed looking stupid as fuck. It didn't matter who she was on the phone with though because if I found out somebody else helped her dumb ass they was going to get fucked up too.

"Alright, but let me find out you touched her shit, and I'm going to go across yo head. I swear you a simple ass bitch." I turned around, and walked right out the house. For some reason, I found myself in front of Sparkle's door. I shot her a quick text. I didn't know if she was home or not, but I needed to see her.

Me: Open the door

Wifey: Leave me alone Quentin!

Me: Man open the door before I kick this bitch down

I was getting tired of playing these back and forth games with her. I guess she got the message cause I heard the locks clicking. When she opened up I saw that she had just got out of the shower. She had on just a towel, and her hair was wet.

"What?" she asked. I pushed past her, and went straight to her room. As I walked to the back of her apartment she was yelling at me, and telling me I couldn't just walk in her house. I figured since she still had to get dressed it wasn't any point of me sitting in the living room by myself. She walked in the room with an attitude.

"You can't be coming over here harassing me whenever you feel like it. I don't pop up at your spot so respect me, and not just be popping up, trying to kick people out of my house, stop telling me what to do, oh and don't threaten to kick my fucking door in. I didn't move here for that shit."

Her sexy ass was turning red from anger, but it was making me happy just being in her presence. I just wished she would fall back, and let me love her the way I knew she deserved to be.

"Calm the fuck down, and get dressed before I bend yo lil ass over." She rolled her eyes, and walked into her closet.

"On some real shit I came here to apologize to you. I was wrong for what I did, and that shit should have never happened. If it makes you feel better, I was thinking of you the whole time." I chuckled cause I knew that shit wasn't going to make the situation better, but hey it was my truth. I walked in the closet behind her, and wrapped my arms around her.

"I miss you ma. Will you forgive a nigga?" I felt her tense up, but I held her anyway. I wasn't leaving here until she forgave me. She turned her head to the side so that she could look at me, but she didn't speak. I saw the hurt in her eyes. No matter how much she claimed she wasn't bothered by me messing with Brittany I knew she was.

"Let's go get something to eat." This shipment I was expecting was going to be here soon, but I wanted to make things right with Sparkle before I did anything else or my day wasn't going to be right.

"I'm not going anywhere with yo lying ass. So where is your bitch anyway?" I couldn't believe she was still on this dumb shit after I had just said sorry.

"Look ma what do I have to do to make you forgive me?" At this point I was willingly to do whatever to get shorty back.

"That's simple, get rid of that bitch." I turned her around so that I could see her face, and when I did I saw the seriousness in her eyes.

"Do you know what you are asking me to do? You are asking me to not just put Brittany out, but to put my seed out on the streets, and I can't do that." Ok was all she said.

"What the fuck does that mean?" Her saying that shit pissed me off instantly. Like I knew she gave a fuck about the whole situation, but she was hiding that shit good as fuck.

"It means exactly what it sounds like. Ok. I'm not asking you to put your child out, but I can't be with a nigga that lives with another bitch. You got pussy at your disposal, and I can't rock with that. The ball is in your court so holla at me when you figure out what you gone do."

I walked out of the closet at a loss for words. I went in her living room, and sat on the couch. I had to figure some shit out, and asap because I wanted to see my seed on the regular, and I wanted shorty around too. I hit Nick up with a quick text

Me: Take care of that shipment for me bruh

Nick: I got you bruh. Everything cool fam?

Me: Man...women smh

Nick: I already know

When I put my phone back in my pocket I saw Sparkle standing in front of me looking good with a black sundress on. She had her arms folded across her chest.

"So have you decided on what the fuck you going to do because I have to go get a new car, and don't have time for your mess." Her ass was really trying to boss up on me, but I'm going to let that shit slide.

"Come here." I said as I motioned for her to come to me with my finger. At first she was reluctant, but eventually she walked over to me, and I sat her on my lap.

"Look I will get you a new whip, but can you rock with a nigga while I figure out how to fix this shit with Brittany. If you want, you can stay with me every night to make sure ain't shit happening.

"I was serious about her stating with me. I was never the type of man to have a female living with him, but for her I would do anything. Like I said before the only reason Brittany is at my house is because I want my daughter around, and that's it.

"Nah I can buy my own ride. and I'm not about to keep tabs on no grown ass man. If I can't trust you from a distance I don't need to be with you." She had me thinking hard as a motherfucker.

What she was saying was some real shit. and for her to be as young as she was I had to admire her maturity. I leaned in, and kissed her neck. Whenever I'm near her lil sexy ass I have to touch her. At first. she resisted, but quickly relaxed.

Once I heard a moan escape her mouth I knew I had her back. I put my hand under dress, and to my amusement she didn't have on any panties. or bra. Her wetness quickly covered my fingers as I played with her soft spot. She started moving her hips, and moaning. Then out of nowhere she pushed my hand from under her dress.

"I can't keep going back and forth with you. We can move forward once you handle your situation. Until then we can be cool." She hopped up. and held the front door open letting me know it was time for me to bounce.

Once we exited her crib Brittany was walking out of out of my apartment. When she saw Sparkle locking up, and leaving next to me I saw the rage building up in her eyes. I knew she was going to flip knowing that Sparkle lived here, but fuck it Brittany not my bitch, and I'm tired of trying to protect her feelings. Trying to protect her feelings was interfering with what I was trying to build with Sparkle.

"So, I guess you didn't learn your lesson when I fucked up your car. Stay away from my man." Sparkle looked at me, and then looked back at Brittany."

Before I could even get in the middle of them Sparkle leaped over and punched Brittany in the eye. I yanked her lil ass up, and pushed her in my house. I closed the door behind me.

"Look Brittany you need to grow your childish ass up. We not together so stop putting that shit out there. As a matter of fact you gotta bounce. I will give you a week to find somewhere to go. Mya can stay with me until you get your shit together, but this ain't working." I had been trying to be nice, but this was the last straw.

"Fuck that nigga. I will keep my own damn baby. What the fuck I look like letting you play house with that bitch, and my baby? I will die before I let that shit happen, and don't worry about me being here longer than a week cause that's all the time I need."

"Open this door Quentin! I'm fucking her up I swear."
Sparkle was flipping out, but I couldn't blame her. She has never
done anything to Brittany for her to have been fucking up her car.

"Calm yo ass down, and then I will let you out. Brittany you
need to dip." Brittany shook her head at me, then slapped the shit out
of me and walked away. One thing I didn't do was put my hands on
females, but this bitch was pushing it. I knew it was going to be
some more shit, but I will deal with that when the time comes.

I walked in my apartment, and Sparkle was pacing back, and
forth in the living room. I tried to touch her, and she throw her hands
up as if I had that pack or something.

"Don't touch me. I have been going through hell since I met
you. I have never fought over a nigga, and here I am fighting this
bitch every time I see her because you playing with people's feelings
and shit. I need to go, and clear my head. I'll see you around." She
picked up her purse and walked out the door.

At that moment I just knew I lost her for good. Everything
she said was true. She had been fighting Brittany, and it was because
of me. I had to respect her decision.

Chapter 7: Sparkle

"Please come pick me up now!" I yelled in the phone as I got on the elevator. I pray to God Tiffany gets here before I decided to go back upstairs, and kill Q's ass. If I would have known I would be going through all this bullshit at Chris's party I would have never danced with his ass. It took Tiffany about ten minutes to get to the building, and when she did I hopped in slamming the door.

"Damn bitch don't take your anger out on my door. Who pissed you off this time?" I knew I was wrong for slamming her car door, but my adrenaline got the best of me.

"My bad boo. So last night when we left the skate party I walked outside, and my car had hoe spray painted on the sides. Steve took me home, and Q came beating on the door telling me I need to make him leave. Then this morning when I was taking a shower he text me telling me to open the door, or he was going to kick my door in. I let his dumb ass in. He gets to talking about how he wants to be with me, and I should trust him." I looked over at Tiffany and her mouth was wide open.

"Bitch that nigga is crazy." She was trying to take in all the tea I was spilling, but the tea was about to get hotter.

"That's not all. We leave my house just as Brittany is leaving his. She gets to saying I didn't learn my lesson when she fucked up my car. Before I knew it, I blacked out and hit the bitch. Q got me off of her, and pushed me in his crib. When he finally decided to let me out the bitch was gone, and I had told him I'm done fucking with him. I swear Tiffany I can't keep doing this." I said as tears started falling down my face.

My feelings were hurt, and I was mad at myself for giving myself to him just for him to turn around and break my heart.

"You tell that nigga I'm beating his bitch's ass when I see her, and if he got a problem with it I will shoot his tall ass. He got my friend over here crying, and shit. Nick I'm not playing you better tell his ass NOW!" I couldn't believe Tiffany ass had called Nick that damn fast. I knew she would be hot when I told her, but not this mad. She looked at me and wiped the tears off my face.

"Don't worry sis I'm going to drag that bitch when I see her. Wait til I tell Keisha she is going to go crazy."

Laying across Keisha's bed I listened to them talk about our problems. I wasn't in the mood to talk so I just listened to them. Tiffany was telling us how she found some panties in Nick's bed the other night, and when she comforted him about it he claimed they were hers. Keisha said that her, and Roderick was still kicking it, but he wanted a relationship so they always ended up arguing.

"So what you wanna do about this whole situation Spark?" Sasha asked. In my heart I knew she was talking about fighting, but I was over fighting for Q or any other man.

"I'm ready to get the fuck up out of here. I feel like these walls are closing in on me." My heart was heavy, and I wanted to cry every five minutes. I still didn't have a car, and I could have paid for a new paint job, but I wanted a car that nobody knew was mine until they saw me get out of it. No more surprise paint jobs, or bricks through my window.

"Shid where we going? Bottom's Up, Pink Slip, or Knockouts?" I'm ready to shake something. Keisha was so serious. "No bitch, I'm ready to leave this city, this state, this country. If y'all want y'all can come, but I'm leaving tonight." I couldn't take it anymore the tears started running down my face.

"Bestie you know I'm down." Tiffany said, and Keisha agreed. I got on Keisha's computer, and booked our flight, and hotel rooms. I wasn't taking shit, but a suitcase with swimsuits, and a few dresses. Everything else I would buy when we touched down.

We landed in Montego Bay Jamaica, and I felt the weight of the world lifted off my shoulders. We checked into our room, and put on our swimsuits. I just wanted to lay by the ocean, and relax.

We had laid on the beach for hours. For the most part I didn't speak. I just watched my girls kick it, and listened to them talk about different shit they had going on. Somewhere from them laughing, and playing in the water I fell asleep.

When I woke up the sun was setting. It was the perfect backdrop for a picture, and of course I wasn't going to pass that up for nothing in the world. I pulled out my phone and snapped a picture of me with the ocean behind me. I captioned it *After a stressful few months I found peace in Jamaica. #NeverWant2Leave.*

Looking down at my phone I saw that the pool party that came with our travel package was about to start.

"Pool party in like an hour. If we plan on going we need to go get ready now." I told my girls as I started getting my stuff together to leave the beach.

"I got some of the best ganja around pretty ladies." We turned to see a Jamaican man standing there holding a pole with bags of weed connected to it.

"How much for that bag?" Keisha asked the guy while pointing to a big ass bag of weed. "65 Jamaican dollars for you." He said.

"Cool let me get it. What's your name though."

"The name is Julio."

"Well Julio here is the 65, and give me your number too. We will be here for a few days, and I plan on staying high the entire time so I need your phone number so that I can reup." He gave her the number, and we left.

After I showered, and threw on another swimsuit I laid across the bed and went through my Instagram notifications. Keisha, and Tiffany had gone down to the restaurant to get some food while I showered. So I was waiting on them to get back.

My picture from the beach had over 1,000 likes, and so many comments. Mostly saying cute, nice pic, or some shit like that. I saw that Q left a comment saying I looked beautiful, and to call him. I logged off and decided to call him to see what he wanted. I wanted to hang up with every ring, but my finger wouldn't press end.

"Hello. Sparkle?" My heart skipped a beat when I heard his voice come through the phone.

"What do you want Q?" I was trying so hard to fight back the tears that were building up in my eyes.

"Listen. I'm sorry for how things went down. Except for that one time I have kept it one hundred with you. I choose you. I told her she has a week to leave, and I mean it. I don't even plan on going back there until I know she's gone.

A nigga feel empty without you though. I can't focus on shit when you aren't talking to me. Yo lil ass came in my life and shook shit up, and I like that for real. I will replace your car. I honestly didn't know it was her doing that shit until earlier."

Wiping the tears from my eyes as he spoke. I missed him too, and it was killing me that I was so weak when it came to him

"Hello, are you there babe?" I heard the panic in his voice as he spoke.

"I didn't hang up" I said in a low tone. I didn't want him to know he had me crying again.

"Why did you leave without telling anyone? I went to your mom's spot looking for you, and I thought she was going to kick my ass" he said laughing.

"Yeah well she's still pretty pissed off she caught us fucking in her house" I told him. I couldn't believe he went looking for me.

"I will be back in the states in a few days we can talk then. I really need time to think about everything." Hopefully he understood where I was coming from. I just needed a break from the craziness even if it is for just a few days.

"Well can you at least unblock me so that I can check up on you, and make sure you're okay?" I forgot that I had even blocked him from my phone.

"Yeah I can do that. Bye Q." I hung up before he had the chance to object. I sat there for a few more minutes in deep thought until my besties came back, we headed to the pool party, and kicked it with the rest of the tourists.

"This week went by entirely too fast," Tiffany said as we waited for our luggage at baggage claim.

"I know bitch the weed there was off the chain," Keisha said.

I was happy to be back because I had business to attend to.

Starting with buying me a new car. Well I just need to sign off on the paperwork because I took care of everything else while I was in Jamaica. My birthday was in a few days, and the first semester of school started in a week. Keisha drove me home, and didn't even wait for me to walk in the building before she sped off. I guess I wasn't the only one tired.

When I walked in my apartment I dropped my luggage by the door, and opened my balcony door to let some fresh air in. I went to my couch and threw my head back. Facetime on my phone was ringing so I answered it.

"What's sup sexy?" Q said with a big ass grin on his face.

"Nothing much just sleepy. What you doing?" I asked.

"Nothing I was missing you so I hit you up. Why does it look like you're at home? I thought you wasn't coming back until tomorrow." I could see the confusion in his face. If I wasn't so tired it would have been funny.

"Nah we came back today. I'm just getting in a little while ago.

"Well come down to my apartment I have something I want to give you." Whatever it was could wait I was too tired to go anywhere.

"Q can it wait? I'm just getting in, and I'm tired."

"Grab you a change of clothes, and come on. You can chill down here wit me today."

"A'ight" I said before hanging up. I grabbed an oversized t shirt, some boy shorts, and headed out. When I got to his door I walked right in since the door was slightly opened. I knew Brittany was still there because she asked him if he would give her another week, but I didn't care. The bitch didn't care about fucking up my car so I wasn't going to care about fucking her baby daddy around her every chance I got.

When I got all the way in he greeted me with a hug and a kiss on the cheek.

"Go get comfortable, and I will be waiting right here when you get back." I could tell he was trying his hardest to make things right, but he should have started tomorrow cause I was too tired to play nice. I walked in his room, and got in the shower.

The hot water felt so calming as it hit my body. I stood there for a minute, and enjoyed the feeling. I grabbed my Dove body wash, and took a shower. When I got out the shower I went in his room to get myself together. I put on some of my scented lotion, and slid on my boy shorts, and shirt. His bed felt so soft, and his sheets looked even better. I pulled the sheets back, and laid down. Just that quick I was out like a light.

Chapter 8: Q

It was taking Sparkle forever to get out the shower. I wanted to have a serious talk before we chilled. I needed to tell her that Brittany would be here longer than expected. She asked for an extra week so that she could move back in her spot once they were done remodeling it, but I found out she lost her apartment, and I didn't have it in me to put her out on the streets.

She was working, and trying to stack her money for a new spot, so I was willing to let her stay until she figured out her next move. I knew Sparkle wasn't going to be feeling that, but I needed to tell her since she agreed to try, and make shit work with me. I walked back to my room. I didn't hear any water running so I slowly pushed the door opened. Sparkle was in my bed looking like a straight angel. I had planned on cooking, but fuck it. I slid my clothes off, and got in the bed with her. I wrapped my arms around her, and got lost in my thoughts as I drifted off to sleep.

When I woke up she was still asleep. I sat there and looked at her beauty for a moment. She looked so good I had to taste her. I slid under the covers, and used my fingers to gently push her boy shorts to the side. I massaged her clit with my tongue. It was like she stayed wet just for me. I moved my tongue at a slow pace trying to just enjoy the moment.

"Oooooooo, yesssss daddy don't stop." She moaned as I began to pick up the pace. Hearing her moan had a nigga going hard. I pulled my dick out, and flipped her over so that she was straddling me. I slid her on my pole. She started moving her hips in a circle. The faster she moved the louder my moans became.

"Damn baby this pussy so tight. I love this shit, don't stop baby." As soon as she started bouncing on my dick I had to grab her waist to slow her down. Lil mama had me about to bust too soon.

"Baby this dick feels sooo good. "As she said those words her body tensed up, and she collapsed on me as she came. I was so happy she came because I couldn't hold back any longer. The faces she was making sent me overboard. I held her tight as I released all of my seeds in her.

"Damn ma that shit was official." I told her as she laid next to me. We both ended up falling back to sleep. I woke up to a ringing phone.

"Yo." I answered. Whoever was calling better have a good reason to be interrupting my time with Sparkle.

"We got a major problem at the yard. Get here ASAP." I could hear the worry in Nick's voice.

"Give me twenty minutes." I hung up the phone, and looked on the other side of the bed. Sparkle was gone, but I didn't have time to worry about that. I had to see what the fuck was going on.

When I got to the yard Robert, Roderick, and Nick was there smoking a blunt and talking shit.

"What's good nigga? I know you didn't call me here for no fucking smoke session." My blood was starting to boil cause these niggas didn't look worried to me, smoking and laughing.

"Yo Rob tell him what you found out." Roderick told him. Whenever Roderick or Rob found out info it was always legit so now my ears were perked up.

"So check this shit out that nigga Tim was not only stealing from you bro, the nigga was trying to set you up. So I'm at this lil freak crib, and she sucking my dick and shit. Once she got done she started telling me how her brother went missing, and she thinks her cousins did something to him."

"So what the fuck does that have to do with me?" I was starting to get really pissed hearing this bullshit.

"Damn nigga listen. So I ask her who her brother was, and why would her cousins try to fuck with him. She gets to telling me her brother name is Tim. When she said that shit my ears tuned in.

Well anyways she starts telling me how her brother sells gun for some nigga, but he felt he wasn't getting paid enough so her cousins, and her brother made a plan to set up the nigga her brother was working for, and then kill him." Listening to Rob run down the story had me ready to paint the fucking city red.

"Who the fuck are her cousins?" I needed to know this shit now. I kept a low profile so if niggas knew I was the gun connect that would be all bad.

"That I don't know, but maybe she will tell you. Follow me big bro." We walked to the back of the yard to a forklift. When he pointed up I saw he had some bitch tied to the arms of it.

"Lower it nigga." How was I supposed to talk to this bitch if she was ten feet in the fucking sky? Once he lowered it so that she was at eye level with me I pulled out my .40.

"Look I'm going to ask you some questions. If you tell me

what I want to hear you will walk away with your life. If you lie to me, or chose not to talk I will body you right here. Do I make myself clear?" She shook her head as the tears fell from her face.

"Who are your cousins that is trying to set me up? Where do they live? Where do they hang?" Nick removed the tie from around her mouth so that she could talk.

"They names are Corey, and John. Please don't kill me.

"Where do they lay their heads?"

"They live together in some apartments called Canfield Green in Ferguson. Their address I don't know, but it's the first set of buildings, and the first apartment on the second floor. I don't know where they hang out though." "

"Thanks for the help lil mama. Yo Roderick cut the bitch head off, and set that shit on their doorstep." I walked away ready for war.

Chapter 9: Sparkle

When I left Q's crib I went home. showered, and got dressed. My birthday was tomorrow, and I still had a bunch of errands to run. I pulled up the Uber app on my phone, and waited for it to get here.

When I got the notification letting me know my Uber was down stairs I locked up, and started my day. First stop was to the dealership. After riding in Steve's Range I knew I wanted to get something other than a car, so I called up my mom's old boyfriend Jim that works at Audi West County, and he said he had just the vehicle for me.

When I got there he was already outside showing a car to a couple so I just walked around looking at what they had to offer. When he was finished with them he greeted me with open arms. I loved Jim, but my mom had commitment issues so they separated.

We walked in the building, and sat at his desk. He pulled out a folder, and started laying the paperwork out for me to go over. When I was in Jamaica he emailed me two different types of SUVs he thought I would like. I instantly fell in love with a 2016 Audi Q7.

After all the perks, and finishings I got added to it the price tag ended up being close to 70k. I wasn't at all worried about the price though. See my dad was a well-respected lawyer in St. Louis, and made a shit load of money by taking on cases from the local drug dealers in the area.

So for my graduation present my dad offered to foot the bill of whatever car I wanted.

I signed all the paperwork, and shot my dad a text letting him know the total, and he called Jim and paid over the phone. Being an only girl had its perks. I got everything I want with little to no questions asked. When he pulled my car around I was in love.

My Q7 was cocaine white, and I had them put white 22 inch rims on it. On the inside the interior was black. I had a screen installed on the dash, and voice recognition car starter. I thanked Jim and pulled off.

After I left the dealership I went and got my hair done at Chrissy's Hair Bar. I got it cut in long layers, and dyed auburn. Chrissy gave me some Kim K. curls, and did my lash extensions for me. Once I paid her I went to get my nails, and feet done. Walking out of the nail shop I felt like a new person. My next stop was lunch

with Steve. He called me while I was in Jamaica so we could link up,
but I had to take a rain check. So today we were going to the
Cheesecake Factory in the Galleria. I was so happy when I got there,
and he was already there. I hated to wait for people. We hugged, and
when the hostess came over she took us to our table and left.

When our waitress came over to greet us I was ready to turn
around and walk back out. "Hi, I'm Brittany. I will be your waitress
for today. Can I start you off with something to drink?" I was so glad
when Steve asked for a bottle of Pinot Grigio.

I didn't trust that bitch with my drink at all. She looked at
me, and rolled her eyes, but smiled. We ordered our food, and made
smal! talk while we waited for it to come out. He told me that he sold
drugs, but not on the corner. He said he did it on a larger scale. I
didn't care, I mean who was I to judge anyone for their profession. I
took pictures on Instagram for a living.

He said he was single, and that he liked it that way because in
his line of work he couldn't hold just one chick down. I could
respect a man that could be upfront like that. When he asked me
about Q I was shocked. I didn't think he knew him, but hell who was
I kidding St. Louis was small, and everybody knew everybody, or at

least it seemed that way. I told him we were still trying to figure

things out. Once the food came we ate and continued to talk trying to

get to know each other better. We didn't wait around for the bill after

we were finished eating. He tossed enough money on the table to

cover our bill and the tip.

Steve walked me to my car. I told him I would call him later,

and he gave me a kiss on the cheek before he walked away. As I

was about to pull off a black Benz blocked me in. When I looked at

the people getting out I was confused as fuck.

"Open the damn door!" Q stood on the other side of my

window barking commands like always. Nick and Roderick stood to

the side laughing. I opened the door and rolled my eyes at his ass.

"Oh I see your baby mama called you. "I knew that she had

called him because there was no way he knew where I was.

"So you still talking to that nigga! Are you fucking him?" I bust out

laughing. This nigga was on one today.

"Answer the fucking question. Are you giving that nigga my

pussy?" He knew he could push my buttons acting like he owned

me.

"No Q, damn! We just had lunch, and talked that's all." He

turned to his boys, dapped them up, and walked around to the passenger side.

When he got in I was texting Tiffany to tell her to check her nigga for bringing Q up here to show his ass. I threw my phone in my lap, and pulled off. When we got to the red light my phone chimed. I looked at it, and saw it was a text from Steve.

Steve: Thanks for coming to lunch with me today. I enjoyed being in your presence.

I was trying to hide my smile, but couldn't. I was smiling hard as hell.

Me: No problem I had fun.

"I see you trying to get yo ass beat today. Keep playing with me if you want Sparkle." I didn't even think he noticed what I was doing since he had his head in his phone since he got in my truck.

"You goosing for real Q."

"Nah yo hot ass goosing, and why do you got on that dress if you knew you were having lunch with that nigga? I bet yo ass don't have on panties either." He reached over and left my dress.

"Exactly! Yo ass parading around here like you don't got a nigga. Dead that shit with him, and I mean that shit." He had one more time to demand I do something, and I was going to slap some sense into him.

"Okay damn I didn't know I had two daddies." He was really getting carried away with this argument. When we pulled up to the apartments he started barking off demands again.

"You staying at my crib tonight so go get some clothes and whatever else you need." I didn't say anything to him. Instead I headed to my apartment, and grabbed everything I needed.

When I got back to his apartment he was walking out the door. He said he had to make a quick run, and he would be back in twenty minutes. I locked up once he left, and went to his room to take a shower.

When I got out I lotioned my body down, and threw on some biker shorts, and a cami. I grabbed my MacBook out of my overnight bag, and went to the living room. I needed to find another apartment if we were going to make this relationship work. Living so close to him, he could keep tabs on my every move, and I wasn't feeling that at all. I mean it wasn't like I wanted to cheat or anything, but up until I met him I didn't have to answer to anyone.

I found several that I like, but the one that caught my eye was fit for a queen. I called to schedule a tour, and shot my dad a text asking him to come with me. He agreed that we could go look tomorrow.

I was happy because tomorrow was my birthday, and if I liked the apartment knowing my dad he was going to make sure I got it. When I heard the locks on the door I sat my computer down, and got up. Q was walking in with Mya.

She was so cute to me. She looked just like her mom. I just hope she didn't grow up to act like her. I walked up to them, and took Mya. I walked her back to the couch, and sat her on my lap. I turned the TV to Doc McStuffins, and started to watch TV with her.

Q sat next to me, and said that we needed to talk. I agreed with him because I wanted to tell him I was moving out of the building.

"So look Brittany asked if she could stay an extra week, and I told her yeah. I went by her apartment to check the progress, and the owner said that she had lost her apartment for failure to pay. So I told her she could stay here if she gets a job, and stack her paper to move. So far she has been keeping up with her end or the bargain. I'm telling you because I don't want you to think I'm on no slick shit. I just can't put her out knowing she has nowhere to go."

He laid his head on the back of the couch waiting for my response. I knew they had history, and he loved her at one point so I understood him wanting to make sure she, and her baby had somewhere to go. I just didn't trust her, but if we were going to make this work I had to at least try to trust him.

"I'm cool with that. Thanks for at least letting me know what the deal is.

"So what's on your mind?" he asked. I got up to go lay Mya down because she had fallen asleep while I was holding her. I went into the room her and Brittany shared, and placed her in her crib. When I made it back to the living room Q had my computer in his lap looking at the apartment.

"So what you wanted to tell me?" He asked as he sat my MacBook back on the coffee table.

"Well tomorrow my dad, and I are going to look at the

Clayton on the Park apartments." I told him twirling my hair.

"Oh snap yo pops moving in them? Those are hot!" He said as he continued to look through the layout.

"No I plan on moving in them if I like the tour." He jumped up scaring the shit out of me.

"What the fuck you mean you plan on moving?!" He sounded extremely mad, but I had to think about my happiness.

"When I met you I didn't plan on moving in the same building as you let alone the same floor. I can't keep fighting with your baby mama, getting my cars fucked up, or having you threaten to kick my door in. It's just too much." I tried to not sound like I didn't want to be around him.

"You could have just kept it real with me Spark. I know you fucking that nigga. Why else would you move again so soon?" Dude had to be delusional because he acted as if he didn't hear shit I just said.

"I wish the fuck you would stop accusing me of fucking him. I just told your delusional ass why I wanted to move!" He walked to his room, and slammed the door waking Mya up. I went to her room, and grabbed her. I changed her pamper and made her a bottle. She was so perfect to me. One day I hoped to have a beautiful baby of my own.

It was after six in the evening, and it felt nice outside so I decided to step out on the balcony with Mya. I sat there while she played in the chair next to me with her baby toys. I heard Brittany's voice asking Q where her baby was so I decided it was time for me and Mya to go in.

When I walked back in the house both Q and Brittany were staring at me, but with two totally different looks. Q looked like he liked the sight before him, and Brittany looked like she was about to explode. I walked over to Brittany, and handed her Mya. She took her, and stormed to the back towards her room.

Q walked up to me and gave me a kiss. He apologized for earlier which he should have because he really overreacted. We walked over to the couch, and he sat down. I straddled him, and began to kiss on his neck and ear. He went under my dress and cupped my ass. Like a switch my juices started to flow. He pulled my breast out and started to suck, and bite on my now erect nipple.

"Ooo daddy that feels so good." I moaned as he continued to please me.

"Um excuse me, but Q can you hold Mya while I get myself cleaned up, but wash your hands first." Brittany cock blocking ass said standing there with an attitude. I fixed my clothes, and stood up.

"I'm going home. Hit me up when you're free." I gave him a wink as I headed to the door. I planned on him being knee deep in this pussy, and didn't want Brittany hating ass interrupting us.

"Hold up me, and Mya will come with you. She damn near sleep anyway." I smiled as he grabbed Mya's diaper bag.

"Bye Brittany!" I said as I walked out the door, and closed it behind me. I heard her yelling as I walked down the hall. Mission completed.

Chapter 10: Tiffany

Today was a national holiday. It might not have been printed on the calendar, but every July 25th we went all out. Today would be no different. I needed to stop by Nick's house and kick his ass first. That's right he had me so fucked up. I went by his house this morning to clean it for him and wash his dirty clothes, and I found a nasty ass bra in between his sheets. It was my fault though.

Here I am playing house with a nigga that couldn't even make a commitment to me. I washed his clothes, came to his house and cleaned it twice a week, made sure he had a hot meal, and fucked him damn near daily. The nigga still fucked around on me, but that's cool because I know I'm crazy, and he was going to learn today.

I pulled up at his house, and walked right in the door. He was sitting on the couch with Q, and Robert.

"What's good nigga?" I said pulling the bra out of my purse throwing it at him. He looked at it, and asked me why I threw it at him.

"Nigga don't play stupid. I found that in your bed when I was cleaning up this morning. Now lie if you want to. First I find panties, and now this little ass bra. You must think I'm a fool or something!"

"Aye I don't know how that shit got in my bed. Mayb—."" Before he could finish his lie I reached back and punched him in his shit. Q tried to grab me, but I swung on his ass too.

"Nigga don't touch me! I haven't forgot I still need to shoot you in your ass for making my friend cry." Robert was laughing as he pushed me down the hall.

"Chill out sis. You blowing my high." Robert was so laid back, and cool. I was surprised he didn't have a girlfriend. I walked back into the living room, and went to the door. Before walking out I stopped, and turned around.

"Oh you niggas better be at the party on time, and Q don't fuck up the surprise."

Nick

"I can't believe this bitch just put hands on you." Q said laughing his ass off.

"Nigga what the fuck you laughing for? She plotting to take yo ass out." I couldn't lie I fucked a few bitches since we been kicking it, but I never promised to settle down with just one bitch.

"Well nigga you either need to either stop fucking around on her, or leave her alone before she kill your ass." Robert said as he fired up another blunt. I was going to have one of my bitches come to the Pink Slip, but after how she just showed her ass I think I will pass on that. I was going to make it up to her at the party, but I'm still not committing to no hoe.

Keisha

I had been planning this party for a minute now. The V.I.P area was decorated in white and gold. The theme was Royalty.

Everyone was told to dress in either gold or white. I had bought gold sequins shorts and a gold sequins halter top. I planned on shaking my ass tonight so I chose not to wear a dress. Mondays were amateur night, and I was about to shake my ass for a real nigga. Roderick was supposed to be there, but he wasn't fucking with me because I didn't want to be in a relationship. Maybe after I lived on the edge a little I could revisit that conversation. I couldn't think about that tonight though.

"Happy birthday Best friend!" I yelled in the phone as I picked it up. "Thanks boo! I just looked at some new apartments, and my dad paid for it for me! Bitch this apartment is Sparkle 2.0. It has everything in the building. I move in the first of the month. I swear I'm too excited. My only issue is Q, but he is just going to be mad cause this move is happening." I was happy to hear that she was making that move because I was putting my foot in Brittany's ass the moment I saw her.

My boo deserves to be happy, and moving out that apartment was going to be the start. "So what do you have planned for today?"

"Girl nothing at all. I haven't seen Q since yesterday. I think I'm going to meet him for dinner later though." She just had no clue that she was meeting everybody tonight. The turn up was about to get real.

"Well girl let me go because I have to meet up with Roderick. I will call you later though. Love you." I hung up feeling bad cause I had to lie to her, but she will forgive me because tonight was about to be epic!

Q

Today was Sparkle birthday, and I've been out getting her gift together all day. Once that was squared away I went over to Nick's spot to chill out for a minute. What I wasn't expecting was for Tiffany's crazy ass to show up trying to start a damn war. I knew she was still mad because of the whole Brittany situation, but damn Sparkle friends were some straight hittas. They didn't play about their friend.

After I left Nick's spot I had to go see Sparkle. I was still mad at the fact she wanted to move away from me, but I was going to put that on the backburner for now since today was her birthday. I went shopping while she was out of town and got us our outfits for tonight. I wanted her in only the finest.

I planned on dressing simple. I was wearing a white button down dress shirt, some white slicks, and a pair of white Hermes loafers with the gold buckle. I kept my accessories simple. I had on my white Hermes H buckle belt, an iced-out chain, and a Rolex. I bought Sparkle gold bodycon sequins dress from Givenchy to show her curves, and some gold red bottoms. I had a beauty team coming to do her hair and makeup at her house. Before getting to her house I grabbed us some Sandwich Depot, and headed that way.

Sparkle

To say I was shocked when this beauty team popped up at my door would be an understatement. It was a little after eleven at night, and I was just heading to bed. I figured Q was still in his feelings about me moving because he hasn't called or came by. I guess he had something planned after all.

I got my makeup done, and Chrissy was there to touch up my curls. I hopped in the shower and freshened up. While I was putting on my lotion Q texted telling me to open the door. I opened the door, and to my surprise he had his hand full with bags, and roses.

I moved out the way for him, and watched him walk in wearing all white. Q was a sexy ass nigga. Like I said he was at least 6'1 light brown, weighed about 180, and had a tight full beard that complimented his waves on his head.

5588/ I saw why Brittany was crazy over him. He walked up

to me, and gave me a long kiss before releasing his hold on me. He brought some Sandwich Depot over for us to eat, and we made small talk. I told him that I signed the lease for the new apartment, and I moved in on the first of the month which was only next week. I saw the disappointment in his face, but I couldn't keep fighting because Brittany's ass was going to make me lose my freedom by killing her ass.

He told me we would talk about it tomorrow. He handed me a Hermes bag, and told me to get dressed. I loved my outfit! When I walked back in the living room Q was gone. I texted his phone to see where he was. He told me to come downstairs because we were leaving.

When I made it to the front of the building my eyes instantly produced tears. Sitting in front of me was an all-white 2017 Tesla with a big red bow on it.

"Happy Birthday baby." Q said as he wrapped his arms around me.

"Let's go though before we end up being late." The entire ride to our destination I played with the buttons of my new ride. As we crossed the bridge I had no clue where we were going until I saw the lights.

When we pulled up at the Pink Slip I looked at him like he was crazy, but he showed no emotion. We hopped out, and walked right in holding hands. It seemed like everyone was staring. The bitches giving Q lustful looks, and shooting daggers my way.

To my surprise, Q was well known. It seemed like everybody spoke to him as we made our way through the thick crowd, and up to our V.I.P section. As soon as we made it to our section I saw my bitches, Q's niggas, and a bunch of our other friends.

Everybody had on white and gold, and turning up. Q gave me a kiss and went to hang with his friends while I went to talk to my bitches. I really didn't do strip clubs, but I didn't mind coming on occasions.

After a few shots, I was up dancing and throwing that ass in a circle. Tiffany pulled me out of our section, and we went to the main floor to dance. Cardi B's new track was playing.

I need all my money makers bring that cash out

I need all my D boys to bring that cash out

I need all my scammin niggas bring that cash out

Don't you see these big ass titties

And this ass out

This was my shit so I was bouncing my ass, and swaying my hips to the music. When I felt hands on my hips I didn't even think to turn around. I just kept bouncing my ass. That is until I saw Q standing in front of me with a mean mug on his face. I turned around, and Steve was smiling. I knew right then it was going to be some shit. Q grabbed me by the waist, and pulled me into him.

"What's good nigga?" Q asked Steve with hate in his eyes.

Shit fam I'll see you around though." Steve winked at me, and walked away. I was so confused because I had no clue they had beef. When I turned to Q I saw he had his fists clenched.

"I thought that was you boo." The expression on his face softened a little when he looked down at me.

"Don't sweat it ma, but did you dead that shit yet?" I knew that question was coming. I never told Steve that we couldn't be cool no more, but I've just stopped answering his calls, and texts.

"Yeah I took care of it." I lied. He wasn't about to start tripping with my ass tonight. I knew better than that. We went back to our section, and finished popping bottles. The strippers here were cool, but nothing special in my opinion. A pretty, big booty stripper came over and started dancing on Q. Me being the free spirit I was I started making it rain on her while she made her ass bounce like a basketball.

After I got tired of being by the guys I went back by my bitches. I sat on Keisha's lap and gave her a lap dance. She started smacking my ass while Tiffany threw money on us. We were in our own world. It felt good to be out kicking it without any drama. I looked over at Q, and he was lit.

He was smoking a blunt, and nodding his head to the music so I took that as my cue to go over there and give him a show. DJ Khaled's *How Many Times* was playing. I straddled him and started swaying my hips to the music. I was in my zone.

How many times I gotta

tell that ass to come over

I fuck you right

Having you walkin from side to side

I leaned in, and kissed his ear.

"I'm ready to take this party home baby." I whispered in his ear. I knew he was ready to cause I felt his dick rising in his pants.

"Come on then." He said as smack me on my ass. I kissed all of my bitches bye, and waited for Q. We headed out the club, and made it home in record time. As soon as we got on the elevator he started attacking my body. He was kissing and licking all over my body.

When the doors opened we went straight to his apartment since his was closer. He took me to his room, and made love to my body all night.

Chapter 11: Sparkle

When I woke up in Q's bed I felt so refreshed. It's nothing like good dick to get your day started. I slid on one of his shirts, my panties, and headed to the kitchen. I cooked him a breakfast fit for a king. I made pancakes, eggs, sausages, and bacon. On the side I cut up some fresh strawberries, and grapes. I finished it off with a glass of orange juice.

I made sure to leave some for Brittany. I never was the type of bitch to hold a grudge. I decided to dead the beef we had since I was going to be in Mya's life. I figured we didn't have to like each other, but for the sake of the baby at least be cordial. I knocked on her door, and when she opened it and saw me she tried to close it, but I put my hand in the way.

"Look Brittany you don't like me, and I don't like you, but I'm not going anywhere so we might as well learn to be cordial." She rolled her eyes at me, but stepped back so that I could come in the room.

"Look Sparkle this shit has nothing to do with you. Q can't be playing with my feelings like he do. He can't have me in his house, and having me suck his dick. Then turn around and expect me not to still have feelings. We were together for years. Then one day I see him all over you. I was mad. Sorry for fucking with your car, but you don't have to worry about me and Q anymore. I'm moving on with my life."

I felt bad for her because I could tell she was still in love with him. It had to be hard seeing the person you are in love with move on.

"Can I ask you something Brittany? When was the last time y'all had sex?" I wanted to know the truth, but at the same time I wasn't sure if I was prepared to hear it.

"It was before I saw you at the party with him. I mean I wasn't lying when I said I sucked his dick that day, but after that he cut me off." I was relieved to hear that.

"Look I'm not trying to take your place as Mya's mother, but I want to be around her. I think she is adorable, and I don't want it to be awkward when all of us are in the same room together. She nodded her head, and I took that as a silent agreement to dead our issues.

"Oh I cooked breakfast if you want some I put it in the oven." I told her as I turned and walked away.

I went back into Q's room he was walking out of the bathroom.

"Good morning sexy." He sounded so damn good right now.

"I made you breakfast so you need to eat before it gets cold." I sat the tray down on the nightstand, and got back in bed. While he ate, I caught up on Black Ink Crew. Sky was my girl. Her ass always had me laughing. Once he finished eating he leaned back on the headboard with me, and turned the TV off.

"So you really moving huh?" I knew we had to have this conversation so I was ready. Besides I had an idea of my own now that I cleared the air with Brittany.

"Yeah in just a few days." I said as I looked over at him.

I'm going to miss you being so close to me. Now I have to drive to you when I want some pussy." I mushed him in the head.

"So that's the only reason you are going to come and see me?" I acted like I was pouting. "Yep that and some head." He said as he started to laugh.

"I was thinking and maybe you could move there with me, and since Brittany needs somewhere to stay she can keep this apartment. I mean that is if you want to do that." He was quiet for a moment before he smiled, hopped on top of me.

"Fuck yeah I want to do that. As long as I can get in them guts whenever I want."

"Ugh you irks!" I yelled as he put his head under the shirt I had on.

"Stop Q. I need to go home, and change. I have freshman orientation today, and can't be late." I got up and walked out of the room. I had some time to spare but honestly, he had me sore from last night so a bitch needed a few hours to heal.

When I got to the living room I saw Brittany, and Mya sitting down watching TV so I decided to join them. When I sat down I asked if I could hold Mya. She reluctantly let me. I sat on the floor with her, and we played together. Not too long after Q walked in, and by the look on his face it was clear that he didn't expect us to be getting along.

"Alright I have to go." I said getting off the floor with Mya. I handed her back to Brittany, and walked to the door. Q walked me out, and closed the door behind us.

"So what was that all about." He asked with a smirk on his face.

"Just a mutual agreement between two people that's all. Will I see you later?" I was hoping that he said yes. Every day that we spent together I fell for him even more.

"We'll see. I have some things that need my attention." I gave him a kiss, and walked to my apartment.

Chapter 12: Q

It had been a minute since we took care of that Tim situation. Now that him, and his cousins were dead I had to figure out the Steve situation. Steve was the drug connect, and while I wasn't in that line of work just yet I had been seriously considering it.

Don't get it twisted I wasn't pressed for the money because I had more than I knew what to do with, but I could never have enough. I was thinking about expanding, and selling pills. With that came the need to open another business to clean up more money.

My main concern was making sure that my soon to be connect wasn't fucking my woman, that's why that situation needed to be done with. Sparkle told me over and over she had stopped talking to him, but when I went through her phone I still saw texts, and calls between the two.

I wanted to confront her about it, but shit was finally going smooth, and I didn't want to fuck that up. I had Nick set up a meeting for us with Steve, and that's where I was headed now.

When I pulled up to the restaurant my niggas were already

there making sure shit was straight. We never went to a meeting with anyone on their grounds, and all meetings we had needed to be in a public location that way a nigga couldn't try no slick shit, and if he did I had eyes around the entire area waiting to let rounds off. I got out of my 2015 Tahoe, walked up to Nick.

"What's good fam? Is everything in place?" I asked needing to be sure everyone had eyes on their marks.

"Hell yeah! You know we stay ready. Let's do this shit!" Nick was too amped. He was my partner, and has been wanting to fuck with selling pills for a minute now. At first I wasn't with the idea, but after he showed me the numbers, and the game plan he had mapped out I was liking the idea more.

We walked into Ruth Chris Steakhouse, and found Steve sitting in the back. Once we got to the table he stood, and greeted us. We shook hands, and sat down to start conducting business.

After an hour of going over the numbers we had come up with an agreement. Steve seemed like he was all about his business, and for his sake he better be because I had no problem putting a bullet between his eyes. When we stood up to leave he asked if he could speak with me in private so I knew it was about to be some shit. We sat back down as Steve's guy, and Nick walked off.

"So check it, I know you fucking with Sparkle, but I don't want bad blood between us." Steve was pushing it bringing up Sparkle.

"Look fam with all due respect I'm not fucking with Sparkle she's my woman, and I would appreciate it if you cut all communication with her. If you can respect my wishes, and my relationship with her then we straight. I don't take disrespect lightly." I made sure to let him know where I stood about the whole situation.

"Well then we straight. She cool and all, but I like my money better." I was happy he felt that way because I planned on making an example out of any nigga that felt they could have what belonged to me, and Sparkle was mine. We shook hands again, and went our separate ways.

When I got back to my building I needed to sit Brittany down, and see where her head was at. I walked in the crib, and smelled food. This was a first for her cause she never cooked the entire time we were together. I went in the kitchen to make sure I wasn't tripping. When I saw her in front of the stove I damn near fainted.

"What's good Brit, you cool? You not sick are you?" I had to ask cause for her to cook something had to be wrong.

"No, I'm good. Why you asked that? "She looked at me like she was confused, but I was the one that was the one that was confused and in a state of shock.

"No reason just wondering. So what's up with you, and Sparkle?" I know what Sparkle had said, but I wanted to see where she stood though.

"She came to me, and wanted to put our beef behind for the sake of Mya, so I agreed. I'm not a horrible person you know." I couldn't believe Brittany childish ass was growing up.

"That's what's up, but peep game Sparkle found another apartment, and she's moving out of the building."

"Really!" She said that shit with a little too much excitement. Now I didn't know if she truly wanted to put her differences aside or did she have other plans.

"Yeah well she thought it would be a good idea if I gave you this apartment."

"We already have this apartment. What does she mean by let us have it?" Brittany wasn't catching on at all, but hopefully she caught on quick cause I didn't want to spell it out for her.

"I'm moving with her. The apartment will be ready in a few days. Now you and Mya will have enough space, and I will be out of your way. She started sniffing so I knew she was crying. I walked up to her, and gave her a hug.

"What are you crying for? I thought you wanted your own spot." I was trying to console her, but that shit wasn't working. Baby girl was crying a river.

"I want my family, and now Sparkle is taking a part of it. It's supposed to be me, and you moving together with the family we've created. I don't get what you see in her. What does she have that I don't?" Brittany was tripping. I couldn't tell her that she was lazy, ratchet, and didn't have anything going for herself. The truth would really fuck her up.

"Look Brittany what we had didn't work. She isn't taking me because I gave myself to her. I want you to be happy. Go out, and find you somebody that will make you happy. I'm not that guy Brit." I tried being nice.

"So you will give yourself to a hoe that shows her body off to the world, and you think she's good enough, but I'm not. Ha! You are a piece of work Q." This bitch was really trying it.

"Bitch watch who you calling a hoe. That hoe not out here fucking my homies. That hoe not out here trying to have a baby by a nigga with money thinking it's a come up. Like I said I'm moving with her. You can keep the apartment, or not but I'm out!"

I was so fucking mad I could have slapped her dumb ass. I went in my room, and packed a duffle bag. I couldn't stay here with her another second. I walked out the room, and went to pick Mya up out of the swing she was sitting in. I held her for a minute, and put her back down.

"If you move with her you won't see Mya again, and I mean that shit Q." Before I knew it, my hands were around Brittany's throat trying to squeeze the life out of her stupid ass.

"Bitch if you ever think about keeping my baby from me I will put a bullet in yo fuckin head." I let her go, and reached for my phone on the counter. I dialed the first name in my call log *"Wifey"*. While I waited for her to pick up I sat on the couch. I instantly calmed down when I heard her voice.

"Baby where you at?" I needed to see her bad. She had a way of bringing peace into my hectic life.

"I'm pulling up to the apartment now. I'm so tired baby. Where you at though?" She sounded like she was in a good mood.

"I'm at my spot. I will see you when you get up here. I love you ma." I couldn't believe I said it, but fuck it I meant that shit. I didn't want to say it though because she has never expressed that type of love for me.

"Aww I love you too papi. See you in a second." I hung up the phone smiling hard as fuck. I grabbed my bag, and headed towards the door.

"I hate you Quentin!" Brittany yelled as I slammed the door.

Chapter 13: Brittany

That Bitch had another thing coming if she thought I was going to just bow down, and let her break up my family. True enough I lost my apartment, but I did that shit on purpose.

I knew that Quentin would never let Mya, and me be homeless so I stopped paying my rent. I got tired of turning tricks to pay my bills when Q had all this money. I knew he didn't want kids when I poked the hole in his condom.

I thought that by getting pregnant it would keep him, but that was the furthest thing from the truth. When I found out I was pregnant I was happy. That was until I found out I was too far along for it to be Q's baby. He never even asked about it. He just stepped up to the plate.

She's around her real father's family all the time though. I told him since Nick's mom was great with kids it only felt right to have her keep Mya. That's right I had a baby by Q's friend Nick. Neither of them knows it, but I was only fucking Nick raw, and the day Q caught us fucking was the day I got pregnant. Quentin tried to forgive me after, but he couldn't get past it. It was easy for him to forgive Nick though. He said Nick was being a nigga, and that I owed him my loyalty.

The night I saw him with Sparkle I just knew I could run her young ass off. I tried everything in my power to push her away from him, but it seemed that the shit only brought them together. I've been with him for years, and he has never bought me a fancy ass car. I mean seriously this bitch's pussy must be dipped in gold for him to buy her a Tesla.

The only thing he has bought me was my Honda Accord. Here I am driving around in an Accord, and he got her pushing the newest shit out. Him saying he was moving with her is the last straw. I will kill that bitch before I let her stop my cash flow. I did the only thing that came to mind. I grabbed my phone and texted Q.

Me: If you move in with her I'm putting you on child support

Babydaddy: Lmao...Do what you gotta do ma.

Me: Ugh you are so fucking dumb letting that bitch brainwash you, and take you out of your daughter's life. What type of female doesn't want her "MAN" to be with his child

Babydaddy: Call her another bitch again, and you will be a dead one. Stop texting my phone, and consider yourself cut off. Whatever you need for Mya I will buy, and bring over. You won't see a dime from me until I get that child support order...bye Felicia!

I was so mad I throw my phone against the wall breaking it into pieces. I needed somebody to talk to bad so I hopped in my car with Mya, and drove to my cousin Ebony's house.

Thankfully Ebony wasn't at work because I needed to know all there was to know about Sparkle if I was going to get rid of her. Ebony used to be close to her so I know she has the tea on that bitch.

"Hey cousin!" She said as she opened the door. Her smiled was wiped off her face when she saw me crying.

"What's wrong boo." She wrapped her arms around me as she walked me into her small studio apartment.

"He went, and got an apartment with that bitch. He tried to make me feel better by saying I could keep his apartment if I wanted to." I told her through my cries.

"Did you tell him how you feel? I mean y'all were together for years. That has to mean more than their few months." I shook my head as she talked.

"Yes I told him I wanted to keep my family, and that I wanted him. I was cooking for him and everything. He choked me because I called her a bitch." I was crying harder now. I couldn't believe I was losing the love of my life to a teenager.

"He did what?! I can't believe Q put his hands on you over her." She looked just as surprised as I was that all of this was taking place.

"Well he did, and then called the bitch while he was in front of me. Calling her baby, and even told the bitch he loved her like I wasn't right there just begging to be with him." I wiped my eyes, and tried to calm down.

"I need some tea on that bitch if I'm going to get my man back. "I was looking at her so that she could spell the beans on this bitch Sparkle.

"Brittany you have everything on her. She was a virgin when we were cool, and if I'm not mistaking I heard his brother Robert telling my boyfriend that Q took her virginity. She smokes sometimes, and drink. That's about it though. Everybody knows she host parties, and take IG pictures."

This bitch was no help at all. It sounded as if she still liked Sparkle. I had to leave here too before I said some shit that I would regret.

"Girl I have to get ready for work. I will call you tomorrow though." I grabbed my baby, and ran the fuck up out of there.

After I left Ebony's house I decided to go get my hair down. I took Mya to her grandmother's house, and went to Chrissy's Hair Bar. When I walked in it was packed like always. I loved Chrissy doing my hair because she was the best in the Lou.

Her receptionist told me I could go to the back she would be a minute. When I got on the floor the high saddity bitch Sparkle was in Chrissy's chair smiling, and laughing like didn't have a care in the world.

"Hey girl I will be done with Spark in a minute." I looked at her, and gave her a fake smile.

"Okay girl I'm not in a rush." I sat there while Sparkle talked about how perfect her little life was.

"So Sparkle what are you going to school for anyway?" Chrissy asked her.

"Girl I'm going to Wash U. to be a pharmacist. You know I'm all about my coins."

"I know that's right." Chrissy said as they slapped hands. I wanted to throw up in my mouth watching their exchange.

"Girl I love my hair! Are you coming down to the Landing tonight?" Sparkle asked her as she got up to leave.

"Now bitch you know any party that you are hosting I'm in there." Even Chrissy liked this bitch, and Chrissy didn't like too many bitches. I got in her chair, and told her I wanted my hair in a twenty-two inch sew-in. It took her a few hours to perfect my look, but it was worth every second in her seat. Now I just needed to think of a good enough excuse to call off work. If there was a party Q was sure to be there with his niggas.

When I got back to the apartment I found the cutest thing I had in my closet, and hurried up, and threw it on. I called Ebony to tell her we were going to the party, and headed her way. When I got there, she was waiting at the door.

"Bitch I'm so happy you called because I was going to have to ride the Metro link." Ebony was cool, and all but she needed to get a nigga with some money so she could stop catching the bus. Her job at Coach wasn't paying her enough to even buy a damn purse out of the store let alone a car. When we got downtown there were so many people we had to park a few blocks away from the riverfront. When we got down by the river the party was in full swing. DJ Love was even here. He was the hottest DJ in the area. The music was off the chain, but my focus tonight was getting Q back.

We walked around talking to everyone we knew. One thing good I would say about Sparkle, and her friends is they knew how to bring the ballers, and the D boys out. I decided to have a drink, and chill since I still haven't seen Q yet. My friend Kim gave Ebony, and me a cup full of Remy.

When Fetty Wap started playing the crowd went crazy. I saw Q, but he was chillin with Nick and Roderick. I didn't want to beg him to take me back in front of them so I decided to wait until he was by himself. I ended up dancing with a few dudes, and even got some dude name Juvy number.

When the DJ put on Bryson Tiller's *Don't* my heart damn near fell out of my chest. Standing a few feet away from me Q was dancing with Sparkle, and singing the lyrics to her. I felt like shit. I saw the love he had for her.

He never treated me like when was treating her. He never sang to me. He just acted like a was some side chick, or something. I watched them walk up the steps of the Arch. When they got to the middle he sat her on his lap. I wanted to throw that bitch off those steps, but her time was almost over.

Chapter 14: Sparkle

The party on the Landing was doing numbers. Our payout for this event was 20k a piece, and I was having so much fun. This was the last big party of the summer so everybody came out. Me and Q been together for a minute now, and I have been loving it. Q had taken me away from the party for a minute to talk so we walked up the steps of the Arch.

"I saw Brittany earlier today at the hair salon, but she acted as if she didn't see me when I waved to her. I'm not trying to be her friend Q, but she could at least try to be cordial." I wanted him to know I was trying. I knew that Mya's birthday party was coming up, and I didn't want it to be any issues at the party he had planned for her.

"Don't trip off her baby. She's just salty right now. I told her we were moving in together, and she flipped out." The way he said that let know they must have had a big fight. "Look boo just stop trying with her. If she don't want to act like an adult fuck her bobble head ass." I laughed so hard because Q was always talking about somebody.

"You need to stop talking about people before our baby comes out ugly." I had found out a few weeks ago that I was pregnant, but I wanted to wait until after my doctor confirmed it. When I went to the doctor today I was indeed pregnant, seven weeks to be exact.

"Wait what you mean before our baby comes out ugly? You gone let me put one in you tonight?" I smiled at him, and shook my head no.

"Nope you already put one in me." His eyes damn near popped out of his head.

"I'm getting my little man! Baby you for real?" I was relieved to see he was happy about this pregnancy. I didn't know if he wanted anymore kids because we have never talked about it before.

"Baby I'm so fucking happy right now! I love you so much." He kissed me with so much passion. I couldn't wait to get home, and make love to my man.

"Come on baby we have to tell everybody."

We walked back to the party, and found Nick, Tiffany.

Robert, Roderick, and Keisha standing off to the side.

"Aye check this shit out y'all. Sparkle about to have my son." He was saying it like he had confirmation that the baby was a boy. Everybody congratulated us, and hugged me. Out of nowhere Brittany slapped the shit out of Q and I was on her ass.

I pulled her back by her weave, and punched that bitch in the face. I was so tired of her miserable ass. Nick pulled me off her. Q and Roderick dragged Brittany off somewhere. Somebody started shooting, and people started running in every direction causing me to fall hard on my ass.

Tiffany and Keisha helped me up, and when we were in the parking lot we got in our cars, and left. Keisha was trying to make me go to the hospital just to make sure everything was okay, but I refused. Keisha was coming back to my apartment to help me pack because I was supposed to move in two days, and start school. When we got to my apartment I took a quick shower, and came back out to start packing.

Keisha had been calling Roderick's phone all night, but he never answered. Q never called nor did he come by so I just packed as much as I could before I passed out on the couch. When I woke up I was the only person here. Keisha sent me a text saying she went home, and for me to call her when I woke up. Honestly I didn't feel like talking to anyone though.

From this point forward I was cutting myself off from the world. I was going to focus on myself for a change, and when I got myself together I would worry about everyone else. I decided to call the new apartment to see if I could move in today. To my surprise, they agreed. I arranged for a moving service to finish my packing, and had a tow truck bring my truck to the building.

I had lost myself this whole summer to fighting, and bullshit I hadn't taken the time to reflect on my life. Here I am a nineteen-year-old pregnant college student. I was messing with a dude that had baby mama issues, and to top it off I felt like I didn't know who I was anymore.

I was happy I hadn't shown anyone where I lived. They knew the building, but I informed concierge not to release my address to anyone. I had all of my mail sent to a P.O. Box, and requested that my name not be posted on the mailbox. I knew it would be hard cutting everyone off, but it was for the best. Everybody had been blowing my line up since I sent a group to all of my friends, and to Q and his friends letting them know I needed my space, and I was fine. I told them I would get in contact with them once I figured out what I wanted out of life.

Once the movers unpacked all my things, I took a shower, and went to sleep. I had been spotting since the fall last night, but I didn't think much of it until I woke up laying in a pool of my own blood. I took another shower, and headed to the hospital. The ER doctor informed me that I lost my baby. I was sad, but it had to be for the best. I did what I always did when I wanted to keep a memory whether good or bad. I wrote a note, and posted it to Instagram.

For as long as I could remember I have done what I wanted when I wanted to without thinking of the consequences. The bible says When I was a child, I spoke as a child, I understood as a child, I thought as a child: but when I became a woman, I put away childish things. That could not be said any better. Three weeks ago, I found out I would be a mother. I started to get my life together, but the moment I decided to partake in childish things my joy was taken away from me. I lost a precious child. Not just because of my ways, but hate, envy, and bitterness were all things that played a part of this great loss. I may have not planned on having a child, but it was

coming. When new life is created, it is an amazing gift from God. I

ask that everyone gives me space as I grieve, and learn how to grow

was a woman.

Love, Sparkle

Once I was discharged I drove back to my apartment. I

needed to get some rest because classes start tomorrow, and I needed

to be fully focused. The idea of sleep was short lived because I

received text after text from mainly my girls begging me to at least

call them.

I couldn't though because I have always been the weak one

in the group. Not physically weak, but more so emotionally. I was

broken so I used my fist as a means of communication. I told

everyone's tea to avoid spilling my own, and the one relationship I

had that was real turned out to be causing me too much stress.

My phone went off again, but this time it was Q. I read the

text, but chose not to respond. I called him over and over the night of

the party, but he wouldn't pick up. Now all of a sudden he wants to

talk. Well now I don't feel like talking so he would have to wait.

Q: Answer the damn phone!!!!

Q: What the fuck is this on the Gram???

Q: So you aren't going to answer my calls?

Q: You acting like a dumb ass Bitch right now…. Fuck it then.

My feelings were so hurt by his words, but I have been called worse so I just have to suck that shit up.

One Month Later

It has been over a month since I've seen or heard from Q. Everyone calls still, but I was only speaking to my girls. I was doing good in school, and finally figuring out what I wanted in life. I had cut my long, pretty hair off into a bob, and dyed my hair back black. I felt like a new person. I wanted to talk to Q so bad, but he was the root of a lot of the drama I had this summer so I chose not to call him.

I was up at UMSL with Tiffany and Keisha having lunch on their campus just catching up. Keisha had finally decided to give Roderick a chance at a relationship. I was happy for her because it seemed like he was making her very happy. Tiffany was still going through it with Nick. They had been fighting all the time from what she said. She really wanted to be with him, but she kept catching him cheating. I knew my girl was hurting because it was written all over her face.

Roderick pulled up to bring Keisha some DQ because she claimed she couldn't think at school without it. I swear that girl was a fool. She said anything to get her way.

"What's good sis? Long time no see." Roderick said giving me a hug.

"Hey hun! How are you?" I was trying to sound excited, but honestly he reminded me too much of Q.

"Shit you know me ballin, and shit. I have a game tomorrow night. You should come with your girls." I told him I would.

"I gotta get up out of here. I have a test tomorrow, and I have to study." I told them as I hopped up, threw my trash away, and left.

Chapter 15: Sparkle

Class had just got out, and now I had to drive through rush hour traffic to make it to Roderick's basketball game. I should have told him I couldn't make it, but I needed to start getting back out. When I made it to the game I had went to find my friends. The first person I saw was Nick.

"Nick!" I yelled over the crowd of people. When he saw me he stopped walking.

"What's good Houdini." He laughed at his own joke.

"Haha...not funny. Where are the seats?" I asked annoyed by his comment. When we got to the seats I looked on the court and saw Roderick warming up. He was really good from what I saw.

I greeted my girls and sat down. Right when they were announcing starting lineup Q, and some random broad walked in holding hands. Keisha tapped me, and asked if I was okay. I shook my head to let her know I was cool. They spoke to everyone, and took their seats.

By halftime Roderick had put up 40 points. I see why he

loved the sport so much. I went to get me something to drink at the concession stand. On my way back I bumped into a classmate name Boss.

"Dang Boss so you stalking I see." I joked with him as I walked back to my seat.

"Nah you must have been following me. You here on a date?" He asked trying to be funny obviously.

"Never, but where your chick at?" I asked not really caring for real. I wanted to make small talk as I walked back to my seat.

"Don't got one. My brother plays for the team so I'm here watching him ball out." Boss was a nice-looking guy for the most part. He wasn't nothing to write home about, but he was an average type of handsome.

"Oh my friend plays for SLU also. Well I will see you around." I said about to walk away.

"How about you come sit with me." He pointed to the set of seats right in front of Q and his date. This was nothing, but the devil trying to make me act petty, and he was winning. "Cool." He grabbed my hand, and led me to the seats. We talked about class, and made other small talk. When the game started back I was in a good mood. Boss was a cool dude. He was 6'2 solid built. He had two long braids going down the sides of his head, and he was light skin with hazel eyes. He was also going to Wash U. to become a pharmacist.

When he leaned over and whispered in my ear I felt someone kick the back of my seat. I turned around to see Q mugging the hell out of me. I turned back around, and finished my conversation. Boss got a text saying he had to bounce so I gave Boss my number, and told him to call me.

By the end of the third quarter I was ready to go, but because I was here showing support for Roderick I stayed. To entertain myself I took my phone back out, and started snapping pictures for Instagram. I made the kissy face, and a few other faces, and put together a collage. I captioned it *Bob on Fleek, Lips on Fleek, Nails on Fleek, Pretty on Fleek. #Slimthick2.0.*

I was back, and looking better than ever. I got up to go to the restroom. When I made it to the top of the stairs my arm was being snatched. I turned around, and was staring Q in the face.

"What?!" Just that quick I was so pissed that he was in my face, but had a whole bitch watching us. That's right the bitch was looking directly at us.

"Why have you been avoiding me?" For a second I thought I saw pain in his eyes, but nope that was just the crazy surfacing.

"Q your girlfriend is looking at you." I tried to dead the argument about to happen, but I failed miserably.

"Fuck her! Answer my question. What happened to my son?" He lifted my shirt up to look at my stomach. I smacked his hand off me.

"Stop causing a scene in front of all these damn people Quentin."

"Fuck these people. What happened to my son?" He was not letting this conversation go. "Well if you must know the night everything happened I fell, and that caused me to have a miscarriage. I'm over it so you should be too." I knew that struck a nerve with him because the grip on my arm became tighter.

"Q I'm ready to go." His date said as she stood on the side of him.

"What's our apartment number?" I had to do a double take because I know this nigga didn't just say our apartment, while he has a bitch standing next to him.

"Quentin please don't come to my building tripping." For a month now I had peace in my life, and the moment Quentin stepped back into my world he was trying to turn it upside down again.

"If you don't give me the address I will shoot every person in that bitch until I find you. Now play with me if you want." He really pisses me off acting like a damn psycho.

"Ugh 1019, and honey you need to tell your man not to come to my apartment trippin." I said directly to the chick he was with. I snatched my arm back, and left. I couldn't catch a break when Q was around.

Chapter 16: Q

When Brittany put her hands on me the night of the party I dragged her ass to my car, and drove her right back to my apartment. I made that bitch pack all her shit, and then I drove her to her mama house. I made sure to take my key from her, and pulled the fuck off.

I got a call from Roderick asking me if I was okay about losing the baby. I didn't know what he was talking about. When he said Sparkle's letter was trending on Instagram I hung up, and hopped on there.

As I read her words my face became wet with tears. I wasn't there for her, and I didn't know what she was going through. I kept trying to hit her up, but she completely shut a nigga out. I begged her friends to talk to her for me, but she refused to talk to anyone. I part of me felt like she was trying to get attention, but I knew that Sparkle didn't operate like that. I had to accept the fact she didn't want to be bothered so I stopped trying.

About a week later I was served with child support papers, but before I was ordered to pay the state wanted to do a paternity test. I was more than willing to deal with the courts rather than Brittany's spiteful ass so I went, and took the test. Three days later we both were told to show up for the reading of the results. When the person said I was 99.99999% not the father I could have murdered her right there.

I had grown to love Mya so much. To my surprise she had Nick tested too, and he was 99.99999% not the father as well. As we walked out the building I promised her I was going to kill her, and I meant that shit. The only thing looking up for me was business since we started working with Steve we were swimming in money.

This morning Roderick told me that he had saw Sparkle, and she was coming to his game. I decided since she pissed me off I was going to bring a bitch around to make her jealous. I should have known Sparkle was too confident to care about the next bitch. She didn't take the bait at all. Instead she ended up making me jealous, and that shit infuriated me.

I dropped the bitch I was with off at her car, and headed to the apartment Sparkle, and I were supposed to be sharing. I knocked on the door, and she swung it open with an attitude.

"Are you just dropping by to keep being disrespectful, or do you plan on talking like you got some sense?" She asked trying to boss up on me.

"What the fuck you mean am I dropping by? I'm at home, and don't you ever forget that. I let you have your time to throw tantrums, and shit now it's time to talk." She had me ready to knock her lil short ass down.

"First, are we together cause if we are yo lil ass can't be running off. Well.... are we?" I saw the tears falling down her face, and as bad as I wanted to hold her I didn't want her to say the wrong thing, and hurt me too.

"I can't keep dealing with your baby mama so no we aren't together." I was shocked she was ready to walk away from me like that.

"Well you don't have to worry about her anymore. I found out that Mya wasn't mine. So will you rock with a nigga, or are you seriously done?" A small smile crept up on her face, and she hopped up wrapping her legs around me. I gave her a kiss, and asked her again.

"So what's good ma?" She had her head buried in between my neck and shoulder.

"Yeah you can be my boo again." Instead of taking her to the room, and fucking her brains out I decided to just take a shower, and chill with her. I planned on having a lifetime to fuck her so I wasn't in a rush.

When I woke up I saw my phone lightening up. I checked it, and saw I had twenty miss calls. I was so tired I sat it down, and went back to sleep. Not long after I was awakened by Sparkle shaking me, and yelling.

"What's wrong ma?" "Nick was shot. They took him to Barnes Hospital. We need to get there now!" She was screaming at me like I was deaf. I was shocked. I couldn't believe what she had just said. We hopped in the car, and was gone. It took us about ten minutes to get there.

We parked in the front, and ran in. As soon as we made it in we saw everyone standing around crying. Sparkle asked what happened, and that's when Tiffany told her.

"I was on the phone with him when I heard a female say she was going to kill him, and that's when I heard the shots. I got in my car to find him, and he was on Lillian and Goodfellow. I called the police for help, and they rushed him here. They don't have any updates yet. He can't die I'm pregnant." I was at a complete loss for words. Nick fucked so many females there's no telling who it was that did this.

"Family of Nicholas Martin." A doctor in scrubs came out of the double doors and said. Nick's mom ran to the doctor, and stated. "Yes, that's us." I walked up to her and put my arm around her shoulders.

"Mr. Martin was brought in tonight with three guns shot wounds. He was shot once in his chest, just missing a major artery. That wound we were about to stop the bleeding, and remove the bullet, but due to the location we had to place him in a medically induced coma to help reduce the pain, and to reduce further trauma.

He also was struck in the head which turned out to be a flesh wound. The last wound was in the leg. The bullet went through the side, and out the other side we patched that wound up, and that should heal normally. Do you have any questions that I can help you with?" Nick's mother shook her head.

"Can he have visitors?" I needed to see my nigga to make sure he was straight.

"Not at this time because he is in recovery. The moment he is moved and situated we will inform you all. Again, sorry to have to meet you all under these circumstances. If you come up with any more questions, or need anything please let someone at the nurse's station know."

We had to wait for another hour while we waited to be escorted to the back. Because he was shot the hospital put him on a blackout list preventing just everyone from visiting him. His mom had to decide who she wanted on the list, and because he was shot by a female she didn't trust Tiffany being back there with him.

Tiffany was taking it bad, and that shit was fucking with Sparkle. She held Tiffany, and tried her best to console her. His mom thought it would be best to just have me, Roderick, and Robert on the list since we were like brothers.

Once we got to the back my knees almost gave out on me seeing my nigga hooked up to all those damn machines. He looked fucked up. His face was swollen, and they had his leg propped up. I couldn't see the chest wound cause they had the covers pulled up.

I sat there with Ms. Martin for another hour, or so and decided I need to take Sparkle home so that she could get some rest while I figured out who the hell was responsible for this shit.

We ended up bringing Tiffany back with us because she was in no shape to be alone. While Sparkle helped get Tiffany situated in one of the guestrooms I went in our room to take a shower. Once the water got hot enough I stepped in, leaned my head back on the wall, and just let the water hit my body.

This was too much for me to deal with. I had no clue where to start. If Tiffany's crazy ass wasn't so messed up about it I would have thought it was her ass who did it, but seeing her react to the news, and hearing her cries for her unborn baby put that thought to rest.

When I heard the shower door open I opened my eyes, and pulled my baby into me. She gave me soft kisses on my lip, and started to travel down my body with her lips. When she got on her knees I leaned back and closed my eyes again. She placed kisses on the tip of my dick.

Then she slowly wrapped her warm lips around the head of my now hardened dick, and began to stroke my dick as she bobbed her head up and down. I placed my hand on the back of her head, and ran my fingers through her wet hair.

"Mmm daddy you taste so good." She moaned as she

continued to please me. She pulled my dick out of her mouth, and lick it from the base back up to the head, and put it back in her mouth deep throating it. After a about another minute I pulled her up, and rammed my dick in her. The sounds she was making had a nigga trying to murder her pussy.

"Will you carry my seed for me?" I asked her between strokes. I had her pinned up on the wall trying to punish her kitty. She shook her head yes, but I want to hear her say it.

"Say that shit then ma."

"Oh my God, Q I'm cumming baby! Stop. Please Stop." She was now yelling and gripping my shoulders as tight as she could.

"Well say you will baby."

"Yes baby, Yes I will please baby stop." Just as she said those magic words I released in her. I stood her to her feet, and we took a quick shower. I laid her in the bed because I knew she was tired. I threw on some clothes I had in my gym bag that was inside my car, and put my shoes back on.

"There's a spare key in the nightstand take it." She turned over, and said. I gave her a kiss, told her I loved her, and left. I needed to get some movers to pack up my clothes, and shit so they could bring them here.

Once I arranged for my things to be moved I went back to the hospital to see my day one. Nick had been my best friend since the first grade at Cook elementary. I caught my first body with my nigga, and we smashed our first bitches together. When I walked in my nigga room he was up arguing with the nurse.

"What's up my nigga. You causing hell already?" I couldn't help but laugh cause this nigga looked mad as hell.

"Bruh this bitch talking about she gotta stick some shit up my ass to run a test. I keep telling her simple ass if she can't get the shit from my arm her ass won't be doing the test." My nigga woke up on ten. The nurse looked shocked like a motherfucker, and damn near ran out the room.

"So you good bro? I thought you was going to check out."

"Nigga I won't be checking out no time soon. At least not until I kill this bitch Brittany." I knew I wasn't hearing this nigga right.

"My nigga what you just say?"

"Yo, you heard me right that hoe tried to take my ass out, but check this shit out she said some shit about killing Sparkle too.

Talking about how Sparkle ruined her life." My head was spinning from the bomb he just dropped on me. I needed to get her location asap before she did some more dumb shit.

"Aye bruh I know you out of it right now, but you need to holla at Tiffany. She taking this shit hard as hell. I'm about to let you rest up. I need to hit some corners, and put a bounty on this bitch head."

After I left the hospital I made a few calls to my niggas, and put the word out that I was looking for Brittany. Next I called my nigga Julio. He was a crazy ass Jamaican cat that had more hustles than a little bit. He was the one who put me on to selling bangers.

"Ello!" He answered with has thick ass accent right before I was about to hang up. "What's up fam" This Q, we need your assistance with some shit."

"Say no more, I'm on the next thing smoking." That's what I loved about his ass he stayed ready for war no matter the situation. I knew Brittany was probably hiding so I was going to take a different approach. Next I called my nigga Juvy. Juvy was the big homie.

Nigga was a straight savage, and a real hot head. It was always good to have a nigga like Juvy on your team. I told him to meet me at our new apartment since I still had to check on Spark, and Tiffany. I also had to make sure the movers didn't fuck shit up.

When I got back to the crib I heard the radio blasting Beyoncé's 7/11. I walked in the kitchen, and Tiffany was sitting at the island eating a plate food. Sparkle was bent over in the refrigerator looking for something. I snuck behind her, and slapped her ass. She turned around and gave me a kiss.

"The movers came by. I had them put all of your big stuff in storage downstairs, and the rest of your things I unpacked, and put away." I swear baby girl was a straight keeper. I'm thinking I needed to come home to supervise them, and my baby was here already on some boss shit.

I looked on the stove, and saw that she had cooked my favorite food. Macaroni and cheese, baked chicken, sweet peas, and cornbread. I opened the refrigerator and saw a big ass pitcher of red Kool aide. I was a lucky man.

"I'm about to have my nigga stop by to talk about some shit if that's cool with you. Oh Tiffany when you ready I will take you back to the hospital cause that nigga Nick woke and snapping on everybody in that bitch. I think he need his dick sucked or some shit." She looked happy which was a good thing because She didn't need to be stressing while she was pregnant.

"That's fine by me. Let me go put on some clothes. Lord knows I don't want your creepy ass friends looking at me." Sparkle said as she headed to our room.

Chapter 17: Sparkle

It's been a little over six months since the shooting with Nick. He was scheduled to get released from the hospital today.

After he woke up he refused to let them run some test on him, and ended up with a nasty infection that caused them to have to do surgery on him again. Timing couldn't be better because Tiffany was due in the next month or so. Q has been so busy trying to find the person that shot Nick that I barely see him during the day. His birthday was tomorrow, but Robert, Roderick, and I had planned a party for tonight.

We were having his party at the Imperial Palace. I didn't too much care for the location, but his brothers had booked the entire venue. I was just leaving from Chrissy's house trying not to be late. She had did my hair, and makeup for me. I still needed to get dressed, and then drive to IP which was every bit of twenty minutes away from our house.

The theme for his party was All Black Everything. I had went to Plaza Frontenac today, and copped an all-black fitted Chanel dress, some black red bottoms, and a cute Tory Burch purse. I

planned on buying Q a white Aston Martin that he had been eyeing,

but of course his brothers wanted to help foot the bill so we all went

in on the price of the car, and I upgraded his Rolex for him. It took

me just under an hour to get ready, and make it to the party.

When I got there the party was in full swing. I could have

kicked my own ass for being late. I walked up to Q, and gave him a

kiss, and handed him his bag. Next to him I saw the same chick from

Roderick's game a few months back.

"Hi I'm Keeta!" She stuck her hand out at me. I looked down

at it, and back up at her. "And I don't give a fuck." I told her ugly

ass. I turned my attention back to Q.

"So is there a reason this busted down bitch standing next to

you, and why does she feel comfortable enough to introduce herself

to me?" He was standing there with a stupid ass smirk on his face. I

could tell he was high off his ass because his eyes were barely open.

"Chill ma, damn." He grabbed me, and held me to his chest.

He pulled me to the side because I was still mugging her ass.

"Why are we over here Q?"

"We're over here because I want your lil ass to calm down

before you do some dumb shit."

"Who is she Q? Don't think I don't remember her ass from the game." I was ready to smack this bitches smile off her face.

"She was a lil jump-off I was messing with when you pulled a disappearing act on a nigga. I let her suck my dick a few times, and when you came back around I passed her ass to Robert." I was in pure disgust how he just talked about passing her around like she was a damn dog toy or some shit.

"So since you out here getting your dick sucked by these random bitches I guess I can find me a new boo." I said giggling.

"You can get that nigga bodied too, don't play with me man." He just talked about how he was getting her dicked sucked, but the moment I make a joke about fucking a nigga he was about to have a damn heart attack."

"Come on man I want a private dance." He grabbed my hand, and led us back to the VIP area we had reserved for us. The DJ turned the music down, and got on the mic.

"Happy 23rd birthday to the king of the city Q. Yo Q look at the big screen, your wifey, and fam have something very special to show you playboy." Everybody turned their attention to the screen.

Live footage showed the black Aston Martin pull up with a big red bow on the hood. Q looked at his brothers, and gave them some dap, and a brotherly hug. When he turned to me he picked me up, and placed kisses all over my face.

"I love that shit ma. Thank you. I have a gift for you too as soon as we get home." He said that a little too serious.

"Well I guess we will be giving out gifts all night because what I got one for you won't want to pass up." I leaned in, and licked his ear before kissing him.

"I'm going on the dance floor to dance. See you in a minute. I yanked Keisha off Roderick's lap, and like a magnet to metal our bodies were drawn to the dance floor. We danced for what seemed like hours before I needed to pee so bad.

"I'll be back boo. I'm headed to the bathroom." I yelled over the music to Keisha. She shook her head, and kept dancing. I could have sworn I saw someone wearing a hoodie following me. I shook the thought out of my head, and rushed into a stall. I handled my business, and walked out to wash my hands when I was hit in the back of the head.

When I woke up my eyes were so heavy, and my head was

banging. I reached up, and felt wetness coming from a gash in my head.

"Why do you think you can come in my life and ruin everything I had going for myself? Huh you dumb bitch!" The person wearing the hoodie took the hood off, and it was Brittany standing there with a gun in her hand.

"What are you talking about Brittany? You have come for me ever since I've known you." I was trying to stall hopping that Keisha would come looking for me.

"Shut up BITCH! You took my man, my money, and you made everyone around hate me. It's because of you I'm staying in a shelter right now. It's because of you that Q hates me. Before you came around he was showing me love, and breaking bread with me.

Now it's like I disgust him. I have to kill you. There's no way around it. If I want my man back you have to be completely out of the picture." The look in her eyes was that of a crazy person, and I had no way to defend myself.

"Brittany you don't have to do this." I said as I started to cry.

"Nope I gave you too many chances." She lifted her gun up, and pointed it at my head. When she pulled the trigger, the loud sound made my ears ring. I felt my body to see where I was hit, but she had missed.

"Oh don't worry bitch the next one won't miss." The bitch had the nerves to laugh as she aimed again. Just when she was about to pull the trigger the door to the bathroom was kicked open, and there stood Q, Roderick, and two dudes I didn't know. I wanted to get up, but my body wouldn't move. I started to feel faint, and next thing I know everything around me went blank.

"Sparkle if you can hear me open your eyes." I heard a deep voice say to me. I wanted to open my eyes so bad, but my body refused to cooperate with me. I heard everyone talking around me, but I couldn't say anything back.

"Is she going to be okay? How could she be in a coma?" Q was asking what I assumed to be a doctor.

"She isn't in a coma. Her body responds to all the test we have performed. At this point it's up to her if she wants to wake up. The trauma to her head has played a major role in this, but like I said it's is up to her now to wake up." The doctor tried to explain to Q.

Honestly, I was very tired, and while I did want to wake up, and see everyone thinking about the drama I would wake up to was keeping me in my sleep like state.

"This some bullshit! She has to wake up. There has to be something you can do." My body started shaking hard. I knew that touch from anywhere. It was Q's hands shaking me.

"Wake up baby I need you. Please baby if you hear me get up ma." I felt the tears leaving my eyes. I wanted to tell him everything would be okay. I wanted to wake up, and hold him, but I couldn't. I heard Keisha crying.

Then I heard my mother's voice asking the doctor could I be moved to another hospital. I didn't understand why she wanted me moved, but I didn't care either. I was really feeling tired, and even though my eyes were closed I saw a bright light. Beeeeeeep! The sound was so loud.

"Code Blue Room 668" I heard my mother let out a gut-wrenching scream before I could no longer hear anything.

Chapter 18: Q

It didn't take a rocket scientist to know what that sound meant. My best friend, lover, and wifey had just flatlined. I had to get the fuck out of there before I murdered someone. Ever since I met Sparkle my life felt like it had meaning to it. I was excited to wake up in the mornings.

I was even more excited knowing I was going to sleep next to her every night. In just a year Sparkle has giving me a reason to become a better man. Now my baby was dead, and all because a jealous ass bitch.

When we were at the party I kept watching her dance on the dancefloor with Keisha. She looked so good swaying her hips, and laughing with her friend. I turned around to talk to my guys for a minute, and when I turned back around she was gone.

I didn't think much about it until Keisha came and asked if I had seen her. She said Sparkle told her she was going to the bathroom, and never returned. I instantly told my niggas to follow me.

When I made it to the hallway of the bathrooms I heard a loud sound that sounded just like a gunshot. I put my ear to the door, and that's when I heard Brittany's voice. We kicked the door in, and there my baby was on the floor with blood running down her face. Juvy snatched Brittany's ass up, and took her to the yard.

I had Roderick, and Robert pay the owner for all the videotapes from the party. I didn't want the police to know Brittany had any involvement, or connect us to her disappearance. I picked my baby up off the floor, and rushed her to the hospital. I knew she had lost a lot of blood, but I didn't know it was this bad.

Sitting here at the yard my mind just kept playing, and replaying the events of tonight. I pulled my chair closer to Brittany. I wanted her to clearly understand every word that came out of my mouth.

"You stupid ass bitch. You were so jealous of a female that you had to kill her. What were you mad because she was doing something with her life, or were you jealous that you could never be her? Wait you were mad because she was getting the dick, and the royal treatment while your hoe ass couldn't get a pot to piss in.

Maybe if you had something going for yourself, or brought

something to the table maybe just maybe a nigga would have wanted to be with your dumb ass. It's cool though Brittany because I have planned something very, very special for you.

"Please Q don't kill me. If you let me go I will leave town, and never come back. I promise I won't be an issue ever again. Think about Mya." This bitch was really pouring it on thick talking about think about Mya. The bitch didn't think about my seed.

The bitch should have been at home being a mother to her daughter, and trying to find her real fucking baby daddy before she decided to fuck with what belonged to me. She made Sparkle's life a living hell, but it's cool I'm going to feed this bitch to the fishes, and then lay my baby to rest in style.

"I did think about all that shit, but what you failed to realize Sparkle was my world, and bitch you took my world from me, so fuck you, and everything that means anything to you. You better pray I don't find yo old stinking ass mama, and put a bullet in that bitch's head for having a good for nothing ass bitch."

No sooner than I got my words out my niggas came walking to the back of the yard where we had her tied up.

"I see you found the perfect ones Julio." Sitting next to

Julio's feet were two massive Rottweilers.

"I always come through my man." Julio said with a smirk on his face. Julio walked the dogs around the chair where Brittany sat, and then walked back to the same spot he was at when he walked in.

"Come do the honors my friend." Julio said as he handed me the leashes. He whispered something in my ear, and told me to say the word, and release the leashes.

"Please Q I love you. Don't hurt me." Brittany cries meant shit to me at this point. "EAT!" I yelled as I let the leashes go, and watched the dogs attack Brittany ripping her to little pieces.

"When they are done feasting on the bitch, burn the rest of her." I left, and headed home.

When I got to the apartment I started crying. The apartment felt different knowing that Sparkle would never be here again. I went to my nightstand and opened it. I pulled the Tiffany & Co box out, and opened it. I planned on proposing to Sparkle tonight after we got home, but now I will never get the chance.

My phone had been going off ever since I pulled up to the yard, but I couldn't talk to anyone. The only person I wanted to talk to was gone. I shut my phone off, and laid back on the pillow. I must have dozed off because I was awakened by someone beating on the door. I hopped up and grabbed my .40 off the nightstand. I went to the door, and pulled it open.

"If you don't get your lanky ass back to that hospital I will kick your ass myself. My baby has been asking for you, and you in this motherfucker sleep." Sparkle's mom was snapping, and I wasn't understanding what the fuck she was talking about.

"What are you talking about?" I asked her. I just needed her to slow the fuck down, and explain to me what was going on. "Sparkle damn near died, and you ran your punk ass out of there. When she woke up you were the only person she wanted to see, and no one knew where you went, or how to get a hold of you since you wouldn't answer your phone. I swear I don't know why you young people have phones if you don't answer them."

"Wait Sparkle isn't dead?" I was so confused.

"No boy now get your ass to that hospital, and you better not break my daughter's heart. I still owe you an ass whooping for fucking in my damn house." I ran to the counter, and snatched my keys off it, and ran the fuck out the door. I drove as fast as I could. I couldn't believe that my baby was alive.

I ran into the hospital, and instead of waiting for the elevators I ran up the stairs taking two at a time. I got to her room, and her beautiful eyes locked on mine. I ran to the side of her bed, and hugged her as tight as I could.

"Baby I thought I lost you." I felt the tears falling down my face. I have never been afraid of losing anyone until now. She wiped my tears away, and kissed me.

"I love you so much baby." She said as she laid her head on my shoulders. I wanted to tell her what I did to Brittany so that she wouldn't have to worry about her trying some slick shit again.

"Look ma you never have to worry about this happening ever again. I handled that situation permanently. She looked at me for a minute, and then shook her head.

"Baby she tried to kill me." She started crying. "Shhh, I promise you she won't be able to hurt you, or anyone else. Now get some sleep." I sat in a chair next to her bed, and texted Nick to let him know everything. I know Tiffany was probably wilding at their crib.

Hell, I was wilding out so I know Keisha, and Tiffany was. I sat back, and thought about all the shit I still had to do before I could fall back. I still haven't told Sparkle what I really did for a living. I think she has a clue, but I'm not sure. I decided when she woke up we would have that conversation since shit was about to get hectic for a nigga.

"What are you over there thinking about?" I didn't even realize she had woke up. Her voice was so soft I barely heard her.

"We need to have a talk about some stuff." I told her looking her in her eyes. It was now or never. If she found out on her own I knew there was a chance she would leave again, and I didn't want to risk it.

"Look Q if it involves you fucking with another bitch I don't want to hear it now."

"Chill ma it's nothing like that. You know how I own the towing company right?" I waited for a response from her. When she nodded her head, I continued to talk. I could tell she was nervous about where this conversation was headed so I grabbed her hand.

"Well the towing company is a means of cleaning up money for what I really do. I sell guns to people off the market." When I paused, she said nothing so I just finished?

"Recently me, and my guys decided to start selling pills." I looked back up at her and saw the tears forming in her eyes.

"So you felt you couldn't trust me so you didn't tell me. Why tell me now though Q?" I ran my hands over my face because she was taking it the wrong way.

"I'm telling you now because I thought I lost you, and now that I have you back I don't want to keep anything from you. I have to go out of town in a few days so I will be off the grid, and I don't want you to worry."

"Really Q how could you tell me this, and then expect me not to worry. When you love someone you can't just turn off your fucking feelings nigga." She was tripping, and raising her damn voice. Before I could speak her doctor came in.

"It's good to see you are up. We will keep you for another day to monitor your injuries, and if everything looks good we will send you home with some restrictions. Do you have any questions while I'm in here?" Sparkle shook her head no, but I had some so I spoke up.

"So those restrictions don't include sex does it doc?"

"Q!" Sparkle yelled embarrassed, but I was expecting to get my dick wet as soon as she was released so I needed to know. The doctor chuckled.

"Sex will be based on her comfort level. She may or may not feel well enough to partake in those activities, however if she does feel up to it then she will have the green light to. If there isn't any more questions I will be back to check on you later." He stated as he exited the room. I looked over at Sparkle, and she was grinning hard as hell.

"What?" I asked her.

"You are a damn fool you know that? You have no filter whatsoever."

"You like that shit though don't you ma? Are you hungry, or some shit cause I can have Keisha big head ass bring you something." She burst out laughing.

"Stop talking about my friend. Her head not even that big."

"Yeah well it's big enough." We made small talk for a while. She was telling me how she thought I was pushing weight, but she never expected it to be guns. She also said she remember their weed man from Jamaica standing next to me at the club. I laughed because I knew she was talking about my nigga Julio. I saw that she was getting sleepy so I told her to get some sleep. When she dozed off I grabbed a blanket, and laid on the reclining chair in her room.

Chapter 19: Sparkle

I have been home for close to a week, and I have been the busiest I have ever been in a long time. Q had to take a trip to Miami so I booked a few hosting jobs down there with Keisha. Tiffany was scheduled to be induced in a few weeks, but she still came with us.

Since it was Spring break there was parties all day everyday down here. We hosted a pool party this morning, and tonight we had a club party to host. Q, and the guys had been busy with their work stuff so me, and the girls went out for lunch, and to do a little shopping. I had to beg Chrissy to come to Miami with us because I didn't trust anyone else doing my hair.

Our first stop was to Ocean Drive to check out The Sugar Factory. After we drank, and ate we headed to the mall. I needed an outfit for tonight's party. Keisha and I both found a two-piece bandage skirt with the tops to match.

She chose a red one, and I went with the nude color. I had the perfect heels to go with my outfit. We walked around for a little while longer before Tiffany couldn't take it anymore. When we got her back to her room I decided I was going to take a nap until it was time to get ready for tonight.

The guys were going with us so I knew they would be back in a few hours. When I woke Q still wasn't back so I called his line, but got no answer. When my phone chimed, I saw a text from Q.

Q: Is everything ok? I can't talk now

Me: Yeah just miss you takes all.

Q: Wrapping up shit now. I should be there shortly. Love you

I tossed my phone on the bed. I was low key mad. I haven't seen him all day. The least he could have done was pick up the damn phone. I decided I was going to head to the beach for a while. I threw on a cute one piece swimsuit, and headed down to the ocean with my beach towel, and floppy hat.

Once I got down to the beach I found a spot close to the water, but not close enough to get eat. I laid my towel out, and laid down on it. The weather was so nice for it to be after seven in the evening. I wanted to take a selfie so I reached for my phone.

"Fuck!" I yelled realizing I left it on the bed. Oh well I guess this was one memory I won't be capturing.

"Damn you looking good right now." I looked up, and saw Boss standing on the side of me.

"What are you doing here?" I asked him.

"Shit ma, same thing you doing vacationing." He said as he sat next to me.

"Actually, I'm here for work. This is what I call on break." I told him. He was smelling so good, and looked even better.

"Why are you on the beach with clothes on?" He was rocking a pair of khaki cargo shorts, and a white tee.

"Real niggas don't swim so there's no need to wear anything else. When are you going to let me take you out?" I wasn't stupid enough to go out with him. The last time I went out with someone Q showed up acting a complete ass.

"I don't think my boyfriend would like that too much."

"Shid what he doesn't know won't hurt him." Something about the way he said that didn't sit right with me. I stood to my feet, and gathered my things up.

"Boss you a trip, but I seriously doubt we go out."

"Well can I at least get a hug then?" He stood up, and I gave him a hug. He tried to grab my ass, but I pushed his hand away, and backed away from him.

"I guess I'll see you around Boss." I walked back to the hotel to get dressed. I didn't even realize I had stayed at the beach that long. When I got back to the room. The whole gang was in my room.

"What's up?" I asked because I was confused. Everybody looked at me as if I was crazy. "Where the fuck you been?" Q was in my face yelling.

"I went to the beach, and lost track of time. Dang what's the big deal?"

"We gone leave so y'all can talk. We'll see y'all at the club." Nick told Q as he dapped them up, and everyone left the room. When the door shut, Q was right back in my face.

"Sparkle don't make me body yo ass in this room. Who the fuck was you with?"

"I was by myself at the beach Q. Since when did you stop trusting me?" I was so pissed right now.

"I stopped trusting yo ass the moment you came in this bitch smelling like another nigga's cologne, and who the fuck is Boss?!" I forgot that I gave him a hug.

"He's a classmate. I saw him on the beach, and gave him a hug."

"So what the fuck is he texting you for saying that your body felt good on him, and he will see you tonight? Are you fucking that nigga?" Q didn't even give me a chance to answer before he had his hands around my neck. He was applying so much pressure, and for the first time since I met him I was afraid of what he would do to me.

"Answer the fucking question Sparkle!" I couldn't say shit I was so shocked that he had just choked me I stood there, and cried.

"You don't even have to answer I know you fucking him." He slapped the shit out of me, and I landed on the floor. I touched the spot he slapped me, and felt blood coming from my lip.

"I'm not fucking him you punk ass nigga!" I yelled at Q.

"As a matter of fact, I'm not fucking you anymore either." I couldn't believe he put his hands on me.

"Baby my bad I didn't mean to hit you. I just lost it thinking about another nigga touching you." He tried to touch me, but I got up and ran to the bathroom. I locked the door, and when I heard the hotel room door close I went back out. I called Chrissy, and asked her if she could come to my room, and help me with my makeup. I took a quick shower, and when I walked out the bathroom she was knocking on the door. I let her in, and she instantly hugged me.

"I'm so sorry boo. Q just came to the room, and told Robert what happened. Omg! look at your face." I started crying all over again because my light skin was now bruised. I had a red handprint on the left side of my face, and my lip had become puffy. If I hadn't already been paid for this party I would not be going. I sat in a chair, and she started applying makeup. We were both quiet the entire time lost in our own thoughts. When she finished my makeup I got dressed, and we headed out.

I met Keisha in the owner's office to go over what was expected of us tonight. He wanted one of us in the DJ booth on the mic hyping the crowd, and making announcements. He wanted the other person to work the crowd, and be on the dance floor dancing with the crowd for at least an hour.

Next he stated he want us to take pictures with the people that were in the VIP booths. This was an easy 50k for us. I chose to work the DJ booth since I didn't want to be anywhere near Q. Chrissy did a good job hiding the bruise on my face so I wasn't worried about Keisha or anyone else seeing it. I made my way to the DJ booth. After four shots I was in my zone, and was turning up in the booth. The DJ booth was very spacious so I was able to dance, and Chrissy even came up there with me.

When it was time for me to leave the booth instead of going back to the VIP section the club had for us I went on the dance floor to finish turning up. Chrissy and I found Keisha in the middle of the club dancing with a group of girls. That was one thing about my girl she lived for a good party.

When she saw us she gave us hugs, and continued to dance. I saw Q looking at me, but I turned away he had me twisted if he thought I was going to let him puts his hands on me, and just be okay with it.

When the owner came to get us I didn't want to stop having fun. He took us to the VIP booths. The first booth was a few of the girls from the Bad Girls Club. We took a few pictures with them, and he moved us to the next booths.

When we got to the last booth I saw Boss, and a few other dudes and females. The owner introduced us to the group, and then we got down to business. We took the pictures, and headed out. Boss caught up to me, and grabbed my arm. I looked at him, and removed my arm from the hold he had on me.

"What's good Boss?" I wanted to slap fire from his ass, but I was technically at work so I had to play nice.

"What you mean I'm trying to chill with you." He was obviously not catching the hint. I guess you can't be nice to niggas nowadays.

"I already told you I have a man, and that I wasn't interested in chilling with you. Now if you would excuse me so that I can finish working." I looked around, and saw Q walking up to us. I turned to leave, but Q caught me.

"Don't leave now introduce your friend." Q was being real petty right now.

"Really Q?"

"What? You don't want me to hear what y'all were talking about or some shit?" I couldn't wait to leave. I was on the first thing smoking back to St. Louis as soon as I left here.

"Q this is Boss. Boss this is my man Q. There are you happy?" Boss laughed and walked off.

"So that's the nigga you messing with huh?" Q was trying to

push my buttons, and it was working.

"I'm about to go. I don't have time for your foolishness. I told your stupid ass I wasn't fucking him, but instead you chose to put your hands on me anyway. I'm out." I had to get the fuck up out of there before I started crying.

"Look I said I was sorry."

"Whatever Q you are always sorry. Words don't mean shit without action." I turned, and walked away.

When I got to the hotel room I packed my stuff, and left. I caught an Uber to the airport, and paid for the redeye back home. I sat on the plane crying, and wondering what the hell did I do wrong in life to possibly have this happen to me. Every time I turned around I was caught up in some shit. I needed to talk to my dad he always gave me the best advice.

From the airport I took an Uber back to my apartment. I shot my dad a text letting him know I wanted to have lunch later since it was already four am. I took a shower, and went to sleep. Everyone else would be in Miami for a few more days so I had more than enough time to reflect on everything.

When I woke up it was after 2 pm. My dad was calling so I

hurried up, and answered before he could hang up.

"Hey dad!" I was always happy to hear from my dad.

"Hey baby I was calling to see where you wanted to meet. I have a trip scheduled for Miami later today so I was trying to make time for my baby."

"We could go to Maggiano's since that's close to me."

"Okay see you in let's say an hour. I will have reservations under Turner." I hung up the phone, and went in my closet to get dressed. I cut all the lights off in my house, and left out the door.

Chapter 20: Michael

When I arrived at Maggiano's my daughter Sparkle was just getting out of her car. I was so proud of the way she had turned out. She had the drive, and hustle just like her father, and looks like her mother.

My daughter was perfect to me. I never heard her name around town as being a whore and she kept her head in the books. Since she stayed in school and wasn't fucking up I spoiled her and gave her everything her heart desired. I was one call away and she knew it.

That's why she texted me at four in the damn morning. I left her mother close to four years ago, because she was afraid of commitment and loved to nag about the dumbest shit. It wasn't that She didn't want to settle down. I think she just didn't want to settle down with me. I was a very well respected lawyer here in Saint Louis, but what the outside world didn't know about me was that I was the plug.

Sparkle's mom knew though, and she was afraid that

someone would find out, and try to harm her, and Sparkle. Our sons

worked for me making sure that everyone paid on time, and that

shipments got to the right people. Faith would kill me if she knew

that I had our son's in on the operation.

I kept this away from her, and Sparkle and didn't intend on

them ever finding out. Now I lived in Ladue away from the street

life. My house was a mini mansion, and I stayed alone. Since Faith

and I split up I never had a serious relationship again.

"Daddy!" Sparkle jumped into my arms.

"I see you still think you're six, and I'm twenty-six. You

can't be jumping on me trying to break my back." I said laughing.

"Whatever old man. Let's eat cause I'm starving."

"So your mom tells me you had an accident, and almost

died." When Sparkle had her accident me, and her brothers were out

of the country doing business with a new supplier, and couldn't get

back.

"Yeah, but I'm fine now."

"So daddy I'm having boy problems, and I needed advice." If

she was coming to me about a guy, they must have been serious

because she never spoke to me about her relationships.

"He thinks I'm entertaining other guys, but that isn't the case." It felt so funny hearing my baby talk about dating. I still saw her as the same little infant I brought home from the hospital.

"Men are complex, if he feels that way it's because he fears you leaving him. Just keep showing him loyalty, and he will come around.

We ate and she caught me up on what's been going on with her work. At first when Sparkle came to me telling me people were offering her money to post pictures on Instabook, or whatever these young kids call it I didn't like it. When she started bringing contracts to my office, and showing me the pictures. I linked her, and her friends up with a good manager that would look out for them, and my baby has been living the good life ever since.

"Well baby girl I hate to have to leave, but I have a flight to catch." We exchanged our goodbyes, and left. I had just enough time to make it to the apartment. I was supposed to be meeting with some guys from here in Saint Louis looking to find a new plug for their pills. After doing my research on them I was more than happy to give them a shot.

I landed in Miami just in time to make the meeting. I didn't plan on staying in Miami long so there was no need to get a room. When I got to the lounge I noticed that they were already there. That was a plus for me. My time was valuable, and I hated when a muthafucker wasted it. As I approached their table they stood. That was another thing I liked about them. They showed respect. In this business respect was important. We shook hands, and sat down.

"Thanks for having this meeting with us. I'm Q, and this is my partner Nick." I nodded my head and began to speak.

"So my question is why are you in the market for a new supplier?" Q looked me directly in my eyes as he spoke.

"I'm very big on loyalty, and respect. Our current plug seems to have a hard time understanding what respect means. I plan on making him understand exactly what it means, but before I move forward I need to make sure our business don't suffer from my choices." As I listened to him speak. I had made up my mind that I would do business with him, but first I needed to make sure he knew what he was getting into.

"We can move forward with this, but before we do I need you to understand that you can't let your emotions get the best of you in this line of work. Whoever she is she must be very special for you to want to go to war."

"She is indeed very special."

"Well good bring your women to my home for dinner back in Saint Louis. We will finalize all the details then." I got up, shook their hands, and walked off. I could tell Q was the one in charge, but because his loyalty to Nick he called him his partner. I was going to make a shitload of money with these dudes, and I think they felt the same. I headed back home.

I needed to give the rundown to my sons on the new people that we would be supplying. I shot them a text telling them to be at my house tomorrow at seven for dinner. Once I made it home I called it a night because I had a big case I was working on, and had to be at court early in the morning.

Chapter 21: Q

I knew Sparkle was going to leave that night at the club. I had crossed the line by putting my hands on her. Chrissy told Keisha, and Tiffany what happened, and they came to my room that night on some straight goon shit. Keisha was swinging on me, and Tiffany crazy as was trying to cut me

. I swear Tiffany ass could have been certified crazy for real. I was going to have Nick get her tested after she had the baby because I know her ass supposed to be in somebody's mental ward. I didn't get much sleep that night either. I needed to feel Sparkle under me, and with her being gone I tossed, and turned the whole night. I

should have believed her when she said she didn't smash ol boy, but my ego wouldn't let me. Instead I did some punk ass shit, and hit her. I have never been crazy about a female like this before, and the shit was scary. She was the total package, and I planned on making it up to her when I got home.

Nick, and I had a meeting with a connect from back home,

and he seemed official. He was a man of few words, and when he did speak the shit was deep. I found text in Sparkle's phone again from Steve. The nigga was on some disrespectful, sneaky shit, and I was going to body his ass. My nigga Julio decided to stay in the states, and join forces with us to get this bread.

"So what time does our flight leave?" Roderick asked snapping me out of my thoughts. "We have to be at the airport in the next couple of hours." I was ready to get back home.

"Damn bro Tiffany, and Keisha must have your ass spooked you haven't left this damn room since they went Rambo on yo ass." Roderick, and Nick both started laughing.

"On some real shit my nigga you need to get Tiffany's crazy ass tested. Her ass could get a check. She really tried to cut me dawg." Nick looked at me and shook his head.

"Nigga you was dead ass wrong for touching that girl. You know damn well she ain't fucking nobody. You lucky Tiffany missed though because she was talking about gutting yo ass."

When we landed in Saint Louis everyone went their own ways. It was a little two in the evening, and we were supposed to have dinner with Michael around seven. I walked in the house, and it was shopping bags everywhere. It looked like Sparkle bought the whole damn Neiman Marcus. I stepped over the bags and headed to the room. There she was passed out across the bed like she had a hard day of work or some shit. I walked over to the bed, and shook her. She looked up rolling her eyes at me.

"I thought you were going to be gone for a couple more days?" I could tell she wasn't happy to see me.

"Change of plans. We have dinner tonight with our new connect so we came back early. What you aren't happy to see me?"

"Q cut it out. You put your filthy hands on me for nothing, and you expect me to be happy to see you?" I sat on the bed next to her, and pulled her on my lap.

"Let me make it up to you baby." I whispered in her ear as my hand traveled up her shirt, and under her bra.

"Q I'm mad at you so stop." I pulled her shirt over her head ignoring her last comment. I started planting kisses all over her. Like always she released a moan, and I knew I had her where I wanted her.

I laid her on the bed, and hiked her skirt up over her hips. Ripping her thong off I dove in her wetness, and began to feast on her. It didn't take long at all for her to reach her peak, and when she did I made sure to catch every drop.

Once I was finished pleasing my baby I went to take a shower. As much as I wanted to feel myself inside of her we had to get ready for the dinner tonight, and I couldn't afford to be late. When I got out of the shower Sparkle was laying back in the bed sleep. I woke her up. "Get up sleepy head we have to leave in a few minutes."

"Where are we going?" She asked while yawning.

"I told you we are having dinner tonight with our new connect." She got off the bed, and headed to the bathroom. Once I heard the shower running I called everybody including Sparkle's mom, and asked them if they could meet us tomorrow for breakfast. I wanted to do something nice for her since I have been fucking up lately. As soon as everyone confirmed that they would meet us I got ready for tonight.

After Sparkle got dressed we headed towards our destination. When we pulled into the neighborhood Sparkle said that her dad lived in this area. When we pulled into the driveway of the mansion Sparkle asked how did I know her dad. I told her I didn't.

"Well then why are we in my dad's driveway?"

"Wait what? Your dad is Michael?"

"Yes, and he isn't a connect he's a lawyer." Baby girl had to be in denial because Michael was the plug. Sparkle hopped out of my truck, and used a key to open the door. I was in complete shock. I hopped out, and went after her.

Before I could even get in the door I heard her yelling. When I walked in I saw her short ass in Michael's face. He took her by the arm, and led her to the back of the house. I stood in the doorway confused.

"What's good nigga?" Nick asked me. The only thing I could say was bruh while shaking my head.

"Why are we at my uncle's house Nick?" Tiffany crazy ass asked.

"I know one thing if you did something to my friend I am going to kill you this time." Tiffany said to me before storming off.

"Uncle Mike!" She yelled walking around the house.

"Bruh Michael is Sparkle's pops." We pulled up, and she flipped out saying he isn't the plug, but he's a lawyer.

"This some Lifetime movie shit bro." Nick said. I shook my

head again, and we waited on the three-man circus to return.

When they came back in the room the girls walked towards the dining area.

"Sorry about that. Follow me this way." Michael led us to an office, and told us to take a seat.

"So which one of you has gotten my niece pregnant?" Michael asked from the bar.

"That would be me" Nick said.

"Well you definitely have your hands full. I think she is missing a few marbles." Michael began to chuckle.

"So that leaves you Q. I take it you are seeing Sparkle." I shook my head yes.

"I was wondering who the guy was that had her texting me in the middle of the night needing relationship advice." I was surprised to hear that she asked her dad for advice about our situation.

"I will just say take care of my girls. They both mean the world to me, and Keisha also. Now let's get down to business. Shall we?"

We went over the details of how we would pay, when we would make payments, and where we would pick up. Then we headed back out to join the women in the dining room. Her brothers came to dinner as well. Everyone ate, talked, and laughed. I was happy that Sparkle had calmed down. Whatever her dad said to her must have put her mind at ease.

We left Michael's house with the promise that he would not only have a shipment for us, but his blessings to marry his daughter.

The next morning we were moving around slowly. It was raining, and we had been up all night watching chick flicks. I slapped her on the ass. "Come on babe we're going to be late if you don't move faster."

"I'm tired Q. Can you tell everyone to come here, and we can have breakfast delivered?" Her lil ass was being lazy.

"Man go ahead and order the food. Make sure it's enough for everybody too. I sent a group text to all our friends, and told them to just come to our spot.

Then I called Sparkle's mom, and dad telling them to come to the apartment also. When I walked back in the room Sparkle's ass was in the bed again. I laid next to her, and she placed her head on my chest.

"I love you Q."

"I love you too boo." I placed a kiss on her forehead. We laid there talking for a while. She pulled my basketball shorts down, and climb on top of me. Before I could even make her stop she slid down on my dick and started riding me like a pro.

"Ahhh this shit feels so good. I love this dick daddy." She started playing with her nipples as I gripped her waist. I flipped her over, and slammed my dick back into her. I bit down on my lip.

"Damn girl!" Her moans were driving me crazy. I pulled her hair, and kept my pace. Knock! Knock! Knock! Someone was at the door. I got off her, and pulled her back on top of me.

"Ride this dick for daddy." She sat on my pole with her back facing me, and started twerking on my dick.

"I'm cumming!" Once I heard those words I grabbed her waist, and finished the job. Knock! Knock! Knock! Whoever was at the door was starting to beat on it now. I went in the bathroom, and cleaned myself up real quick, while Sparkle hopped in the shower. I went to the door, and There stood, Tiffany, Nick, Keisha, Roderick, and the restaurant delivery guy.

"Y'all are just nasty. Got us out here waiting while y'all fuck." Tiffany said as she pushed passed me.

"I dapped my guys up, and they went in. I paid for the food, and gave the dude a nice ass tip since he had to wait. Once they were chilling I went in the bathroom, and hopped in the shower as Sparkle was getting out.

"Yo you need to holla at yo friend I really think she's crazy." I told her as she got dressed.

Everyone except Robert was here so we waited a little long for him, and his date to come. Knock, Knock.

"About time I feel like I can eat a horse." Tiffany was always being extra. I opened the door, and there he stood with Keeta.

"What's good y'all. Come in before Tiffany eats all the damn food." Tiffany thought she was slick we kept catching her eating, but no one said anything because she was eating for two. As soon as we walked where everybody was the crazies started up.

"Oh hell nah! Who invited this runner?" Keisha said a little too loud.

"I need to call Chrissy. Besides she's late anyway. Robert have you spoke to her today." Tiffany was being real petty. I looked over at Sparkle, and she rolled her eyes. Instead of Robert speaking up he stood there, and laughed.

"Yo y'all tripping." Nick said grabbing Tiffany.

"No he tripping knowing Sparkle don't fuck with that road runner." Keisha was serious. "A'ight y'all let's eat."

"Oh so y'all was going to start without me?" We all turned around, and there stood Chrissy with her hands on her hips. She was standing there with some short ass T Pain looking dude. She walked up to Robert and gave him a friendly hug, and then greeted everyone else.

"Oh this shit about to get good. I should have brought some popcorn." Keisha was dead as serious as she looked back and forth from Chrissy to Robert.

We all sat at the table eating, and talking shit. I was happy to see Ms. Faith, and Michael getting along.

"So I asked everyone here because I needed to ask Sparkle something very important." I got down on one knee, and took Sparkle's hand.

"Sparkle baby will you do me the honor of being Mrs. Quentin "Q" Miller?" She got down on the floor with me, and started crying. I picked her up, and asked her again.

"Will you marry me?" She kept shook her head repeatedly. I

took the two carat Tiffany Novo ring out of the box, and placed it on her finger. Her dad gave me a hug, and her mom sat in the chair crying. The rest of the gang congratulated us, and to my surprise so did Keeta. It felt good knowing that she wanted to be with me forever.

"I think I love my ring almost more than I love you! It's so freaking gorgeous." I started laughing because she was starting to cry. Her, and her mom were so much alike.

After everyone left I helped Sparkle clean up. My phone started ringing in my pocket. "Yo." I answered knowing it was Nick.

"Aye where is Sparkle?"

"She's right here what's up?"

"Bro get here to DePaul hospital now. It's Tiffany." He hung up without even telling me what was up. I told Sparkle we had to go now. We hopped in her Tesla, and got to the hospital as fast as we could.

When we got there, we had the go to the information desk to find her location since we couldn't get ahold of anyone. They told us to go to labor, and delivery. The first person we saw when we got off the elevators was Keisha. She told us that Tiffany water broke while she was cursing out the chick at Krispy Kreme.

We waited for at least six hours before Nick came out, and announced that the baby was here. Sparkle asked how Tiffany was feeling, and Nick shook his head before telling us that they had to medicate Tiffany because she started cursing the nurses out telling them not to put a microchip in her damn baby. I was laughing so hard my side was hurting. I wish I could have seen that shit. It funny watching other people get snapped on by her crazy ass.

When they finally said Tiffany could have visitors we all piled up in her room. Baby Nicki looked so adorable wrapped in the little baby blanket. What looked even better was watching Sparkle calm her down when she started to cry. She walked around the room bouncing, and singing to Nicki.

Chapter 22: Sparkle

Spring break was over, and my school workload was crazy. I was spending more time at school than I was at home. Q has been so busy with expanding his business with my father so the only time we really get to see each other is at night. He had planned us a trip to Las Vegas for the weekend. I needed to relax, and take a load off. I still had to go to the gun range when I left school today.

Ever since that Brittany incident I have been taking shooting lessons, and I have gotten good with my aim. The other day I got a pink .380. I texted Q to see what he wanted for dinner tonight.

Me: What do you want for dinner tonight baby?

I went back to writing my paper. This damn paper was taking a lot out of me, and was due the Monday after we get back from Vegas so I had to go hard now to get it done. When I looked back down I saw I still hadn't got a response from Q so I sent another one.

Me: Um did you get my last text? What do you want for dinner?

Hubby: OUR man is sleeping right now, but I think he might want some steak, and potatoes. Do you think you can handle that sweetie?

Me: Who is this?

Hubby: Oh girl this Keeta......you know his baby mama. We're at his apartment on Lindell if you want to stop by

Me: Well Keeta.... tell OUR man to call me when he gets up

That was all I needed to hear. I was going to kick Q's ass as soon as he got home. I threw my books in my bookbag, and rushed my ass home. If Q wanted to play with me then we can play. I couldn't get home fast enough. As soon as I got in the door I ran straight to the hall closet. I grabbed two boxes out, and went straight to our closet we shared, and started throwing his shit in them. I asked him not to play with me, and yet he had invited this bitch in our house, and now he was laid up with the hoe.

Buzzzzzzz!

I snatched my phone off the dresser.

"WHAT?" I yelled into the receiver.

"Baby I didn't tell her to text you." The nigga didn't even deny being with her.

"Q so what do you need sweetheart. I'm kinda in the middle of something." I was a little too calm for my own good, and I knew when I got like this it was because I was about to snap. "Baby I'm on my way home."

"Oh okay see you soon." I said as I finished boxing as much of his shit up as I could. I made sure to leave him one pair of underwear so he could wash his dirty dick.

I used the service elevator to get to the garage. When I got to his parking spot I popped the locks on his Aston Martin, and threw all his shit on the seats. Once I had the clothes, shoes, and jewelry scattered around the car perfectly I grabbed the lighter fluid from one of the boxes, and sprayed everything inside the car with it. Right before I could light the match he pulled up, and hopped out. I lit the match, and threw it in the car, and slammed the door.

What the fuck! Man do you realize what the fuck you just did?!" He kept yelling as I walked away. I looked over my shoulder one last time as I got in my car. He was on the phone with who I assume was the fire department. Q always talked about how crazy my friends were, but he never thought I could be. I guess he never heard the expression birds of a feather flock together.

Like I said before I hated drama, while my girls didn't mind it I tried to stay away from it at all cost because I knew what I was capable of.

Now here I am pulling Angela Bassett and shit. I bet you I don't cry no more. A bitch is tired of crying over a nigga. Siri was alerting me of an incoming call.

"Answer call Siri." Sparkle baby why would you do that shit? You burned all my shit." If that was his only concern he had another thing coming.

"Is she pregnant by you?" I needed to know the truth.

"Baby I'm sorry it was a slip up, and she got pregnant." I started laughing uncontrollably. A fucking slip up. He sharing a bitch with his brother, and going in that hoe raw.

"Okay Q it was a mistake. I parked my car, and popped the trunk. "I gotta go Q, but look call me back in like twenty minutes." I hung up before he could say anything.

I went to the back of my car, and changed into the clothes I had in my emergency bag. I threw on an oversized hoodie, and then tied my Timbs tight. It was a little after nine, and already dark. I put everything I needed in the front pocket of the hoodie and started walking. The walk I was taking was two blocks away, and I didn't want to have anything in my hands just in case I needed to use them.

Once I got to the apartment complex I put on a pair of snow gloves that were in my bag. I made sure to use the back entrance because I knew for certain it didn't have cameras near the doors, or elevator. I took the elevator to the third floor, and used the key Q had given me a while back to get in his old apartment

All the lights were off so I turned on the living room light. I saw a condom wrapper on the floor, and that shit made my blood boil even more. I walked to the master bedroom, and just like every other room in here it was empty. I walked in the closet, and pulled down all his clothes. I went in the pocket of my hoodie, and got out the lighter fluid, and matches I had. I started throwing the fluid on any and everything.

Once I was satisfied I grabbed the matches lit it, and threw the whole book on the floor. I left out the apartments the same way I entered. I walked back to my car making sure I kept the hoodie on just in case the police check for footage around the building. Once I made it to my car I got in, and drove off. My phone was doing numbers.

"Hello." I answered as if nothing had happened. "Sparkle Renee what have you gotten into? That boy came over here crying, and carrying on. "My mama was so damn extra. I swear I couldn't take her sometimes.

"Ma I'm good, and whatever goes on between Q and me he needs to leave you out of it. Look mom I'm driving, and need to focus on the road so I will call you later.

I pulled up to Keisha's house, and sat on her porch since her street was still popping. I texted her though.

Me: Bestie are you at home????

Keisha: Yep

Me: I'm sitting on the porch come outside

I logged into Instagram, and snapped a picture of me smiling. The caption read: Unbothered #Petty.

"Bitch are you really out here taking pictures after your ass just set it off?" Keisha seemed mad, until she burst out laughing, and gave me a high five.

"Yesss Bish Yesss! Oh, and I'm sure Roderick about to be calling you telling you the rest too. After I set his car on fire with all his shit in it, I went right back to his old apartment, and burnt that bitch to the ground too. I kept telling him not to play with me." Keisha was looking shocked now.

"Girl I knew we were besties for a reason. So, what did he do because you know Roderick ass didn't tell me that much." I told her the story from the texts, and the phone calls.

"Keisha when I tell you I have one more thing planned it's going to take everybody by storm. Q don't know who he's fucking with for real."

"I know that's right best friend. Q called over here too looking for you."

"Fuck him." I said as I looked at my phone.

Boss: Are you still playing hard to get? I wanna kick it with you on some real shit

This nigga had perfect timing. I thought to myself as I responded

Me: Nope I'm not....What did you have in mind?

Boss: Meet me at the Marquee I'm posted up in the booth all the way

in the back

I got up, and walked in her house.

"Do I still have clothes over here?" I asked her as I walked through the living room.

"Girl of course you do." I went in her closet, and found a bag of stuff I left over there. I found a pink bodycon dress, and some black heels. I took a quick shower, and got dressed. I put my hair in a bun, grabbed a pair of her earrings, and some bracelets off her dresser, and left.

I got to the Marquee, and walked straight to the back. I put on my game face and walked up to Boss. He stood up, and gave me a hug. We talked, and kicked it for a while.

Of course I took pictures to put on Instagram. I sat on Boss's lap and snapped the picture. I captioned it *It's about to be a long night *wink*.*

I took one more to make sure I got my point across. I pressed my lips against Boss's and took the selfie. The picture read *Somebody's about to get lucky tonight.* I grabbed Boss's hand and led him out of the club.

We hopped in my car, and I drove to the Four Seasons. I paid for a room, and we went up. As soon as we got to the room I handed him a condom, and pressed record on my phone. I propped the phone up on the TV, and undressed in front of it. I laid on the bed, and let Boss have his way with me. His sex game was whack, but I made sure to throw out a couple of moans, and even said his name a few times.

When he was done I hopped up, pressed stop on the recorder, and went to take a shower. While I was in there I sent the recording to Q's phone, with a message that read *Here's something to go to sleep to.* I pressed send, and waited for the explosion I knew was soon to come.

When I walked out of the bathroom Boss was sleep, so I politely woke him up and told him he had to bounce. I had already got him an Uber so that he could get back to his car.

"Damn baby it's like that?"

"Yep, but I will see you in class." I closed the door behind him, and went to lay down. I laid back on the bed, and planned my next move. I knew exactly what I was going to do, but it had to be planned perfectly. I fell asleep thinking about Q.

When I woke up my phone was ringing, and someone was

banging on the room door. Instead of checking my phone I got up and opened the door.

"Why are you here?" I didn't want to start my day with this drama, but fuck it here we go. "Why you do my nigga like that?" Nick asked.

"Look Nick I'm not trying to go there with you, but you should be asking yo boy why he did me the way he did. Get the fuck outta here with that my boy shit." I was getting mad all over again.

"Look sis you got my man out here looking real bad. He said you set him some video, and then he just started breaking shit."

"Oh so he does have feelings?" I felt a little better knowing he watched my homemade flick. I sat on the bed, and dialed room service. I ordered my food, and then looked at Nick.

"Do you want something to eat?" He shook his head nah.

"Why you sitting here acting like you don't care about my nigga. Wait is that a condom wrapper?" Nick asked pointing to the floor by my foot.

"What he didn't show you my movie?"

"Yo you bugging Spark. I know what he might have done was messed up, but you should never let a man take you out of your zone." What he was saying was true, but I wasn't trying to hear it.

"What he MIGHT have done? No Nick let's talk about what he has done. He has had me fighting a bitch over him. He was the reason I almost lost my life. He did choke me out. He did smack the fuck out of me for no reason. He did cheat on me. He did invite the bitch he cheated on me with into our home.

Oh and he did get the bitch pregnant! So if you want to talk about what I shouldn't be doing maybe you should do the same with your friend because I was a loyal bitch to him through it all." Nick ran his hands over his face. I was so hurt. I know I said I wasn't going to cry anymore, but the shit hurt so bad.

"Don't cry Sparkle. You didn't deserve that shit. I'm not trying to upset you, but Tiffany tracked your phone, and made me come check on you since you wouldn't answer your phone." "I'm fine Nick, but can you ride with me somewhere please. When he agreed, I threw my clothes on, and we left.

As I drove down I-70 I called my dad.

"Hey daddy! Did you get that information I asked you about last night? Good. Nick can you type this into my GPS please?" As I read off the address Nick typed it in the GPS.

"Thanks daddy." I hung up, and Nick asked where we were going. I told him he would see in a minute. When we got to Jennings I parked on the next street over. I went to my trunk and threw on some leggings, and flats. It was just after ten in the morning so I didn't want to look too suspect. I grabbed everything I needed, and slammed the trunk. Nick hopped out, and we started walking.

We both were quiet the entire time. I was thinking about what I was about to do, and I had no clue what Nick was thinking. He just kept glancing at me shaking his head. I told him to stand right where his was, and walked ahead of him. I answered my phone, and confirmed my appointment, and then hung up. I turned to Nick, and told him to come on.

Once we got to the alley we walked through a backyard, and up the back porch. I told Nick to knock on the door for me. At first he was hesitant to do it, but he did like I asked. When the female on the other side asked who was it Nick said his name. He looked at me. "I can't believe you brought me with you to fight this girl." He said as the door opened. I was standing to the side so that she couldn't see me.

SPARKLE OF HIS EYE

"Oh hey Nick. What are you doing here?" Keeta asked. I moved into her sight, and punched the bitch in the mouth. I pushed my way in, and used a pair of latex gloves to close and lock the door.

"Don't touch anything Nick." He looked at me like I was crazy as I check to make sure my gun was fully loaded.

"What are you doing at my house Sparkle?" She asked still holding her nose.

"Oh bitch I came to visit OUR baby since we sharing shit now. Sit the fuck down hoe!" I yelled as I slapped her ass.

"Aye sis I'm not about to let you shoot this girl, and she's pregnant." Nick said too sure of himself.

"You don't have to let me do shit." I said pointing the gun at him. I will take yo ass out too before I let you stop me. Keeta started crying, and begging me not to do this. What her and Nick failed to realize was I had already made up my mind.

"Bitch shut up! You getting on my nerves. I'm going to make this quick because I have a lunch date with my daddy, and he hates tardiness." I lifted the gun, and shot her once in her stomach, and again in her head. We walked out the back door, and ran to my car. I dropped Nick off back at the hotel, and headed home to get ready to go to lunch.

Chapter 23: Q

"Man when I say you fucked up bruh you just don't get it." Nick said as he walked back into the guest room I was staying in at his crib.

"Nigga I know I fucked up. I don't need you rubbing the shit in."

"No my nigga like you really fucked up. You didn't see the shit I just seen." He only went to her hotel room. So I didn't understand why he was making a big deal out of the shit.

"Nick stop acting like you haven't fucked around on Tiffany's crazy ass."

"Yeah I fucked around on her, but she has never murked any of the bitches I fucked." I leaped up from the bed.

"My nigga what you just say?!" He stood there shaking his head so I knew what he was about to say was going to be some real shit, but I wasn't ready for it.

"Nigga she took me to Keeta's house, and made me watch. I told her I wasn't about to let her shoot Keeta, but she pulled the burner on me. Yo she shot her in the stomach, and then in the head." I was fucked up about what he said, not because she killed her, and the baby. I was fucked up that I turned Sparkle into a damn monster. I didn't even know she had a gun.

"Bruh I gotta go find her."

"She went to lunch went with her pops. She didn't say where though bruh."

I ran out of Nick's house, and jumped in my truck. One thing I knew about her was she was a creature of habit. So I knew if she was going to go to either one of two places Maggiano's or Denny's. She loved Italian food, and wanted it every chance she got, but I also knew that she ate breakfast as a comfort food. I decided to try Denny's first since I knew she was emotional. I pulled up to the one on Dorsett Road, and saw her Audi parked in the lot. I hopped out, and went inside. I saw Michael first, and when he saw me he gave me a head nod, and motioned for me to come over. When I got to the table Sparkle had her back to me.

"Please have a seat. We were just discussing you." Michael said a little too calm sort of how Sparkle sounded before she burned all my shit. I didn't know if I was in a good position or not. I sat down, and when Sparkle looked up at me I saw that she was crying. I didn't even try to console her because I wasn't trying to get my ass shot from touching her.

"Daddy I have to go, but I will stop by your house later." She said to Michael as she got up, and walked to the exit. I shook my head because she didn't even acknowledge I was in her presence.

"So how's everything holding up with that shipment you got?" He asked as if I hadn't just broken his daughter's heart.

"Everything going according to schedule, but I came here to try to talk to Sparkle." He held up his hands, and started speaking.

"Look I try not to get into her business. I am her father before I am anything else, so when she calls to vent I listen. What you have done is very distasteful, but I will not judge you based on your personal problems.

That's the business side of me talking, but the father side will say this to you. Since my daughter is headed to kill my grandchild I should take someone you love from you, but I won't because my baby girl doesn't need to have a baby right now. You better fix this shit, and if I have to fix it that pretty mother of yours that lives in Memphis will be burying another son.

"Do we have an understanding?" I wanted to kill this

motherfucker for threatening my life, but instead I put myself in his shoes, and knew I would do the same.

"Yeah it's understood." I got up, and went to my car. Laying my head on the steering wheel the conversation just kept replaying in my head. I can't believe Sparkle is pregnant, and about to kill my seed. I had no one to blame, but myself for fucking that hoe. I'm happy that Sparkle killed her because I had every intention on putting my foot in her ass.

As I drove around my mind kept reliving all of the good times we had together. If I didn't talk to her soon I was going to kill everything moving. I went to the apartment that we shared because I didn't want to be around anyone.

When I got to the door I heard music playing. I opened the front door, and tripped over one of Sparkle's shoes. The entire house was dark, and Beyoncé's Broken Hearted Girl was blasting through the surround sound speakers. I walked to the bedroom, and there she was laying in bed crying. I felt like shit knowing I was yet again the cause of her pain. I sat at the end of the bed with my back facing her. I put my head in my hands, and sat there until I felt the cold steel of a gun on the back of my head.

"Why the fuck are you here?" I knew it was Sparkle talking, but the hate that was dripping from her voice made her sound like a different person.

"Baby I needed to see you. I'm sorry, but please let me fix this." I tried to plead with her. I heard the gun cock, and turned to her.

"Baby are you really going to shoot me?"

"I was thinking more like send you to hell with your bitch, and her bastard child." I reached for the gun, and it went off.

"Get out! I hate you! Here I am pregnant again with your child and you're out sticking your dick in whatever hole you can find."

Hearing her say that she was pregnant made me feel a little bit better. I mean she did just try to shoot me.

"So you didn't kill the baby." I asked her.

"No, but that doesn't mean I'm not going to." Hearing my phone ring snapped me out of my thoughts.

"Yo."

"Aye fam I got something you might want to see like now." Juvy said into the phone. "A'ight give me like an hour, and meet me at the yard." I said, and then hung up the phone.

"Look Sparkle can I make this right please? I gotta go, but I can come back, and we can talk."

"Bye Q. When you get back I won't be here." I walked out of the door feeling defeated.

When I pulled up to the yard I was ready to see what couldn't wait. Like usual I walked to the back of the yard, and saw the gang there huddled in a circle talking. I walked up to the group, and in the middle of my men sat some random ass nigga.

"Who is this clown?" I asked clearly annoyed.

"He's one of Steve workers. Check this shit out. Repeat what you told me." Juvy said striking the dude in the head with the butt of his gun.

"Steve put a bounty on your head. He thinks you stole some pills, and money from him. He said you sent one of your guys to comp from him. You never paid, and didn't have his product. He's offering whoever brings you to him alive 100k." I was in disbelief.

When I started doing business with Michael I washed my hands with that nigga. I still planned on killing him, but with all the bullshit going on around me I just didn't have the time.

Now here this nigga is telling me Jason put a bounty on me.

"So let me get this straight you're telling me that one of my niggas comped some pills from him, never paid, and now this nigga wants my head?"

I couldn't win for losing. One thing I knew for sure was I was about to start laying some niggas flat, and that was a fact.

"Let him go" I told Juvy. Everybody looked at me like I was crazy.

"I said let the nigga go!" They untied him, and as soon as he got up to walk away I put a bullet between his eyes. I was ready for war, and niggas mamas, kids, girlfriends, and dogs were about to come up missing.

"I want all ears to the street to find out who got work from Steve, and when y'all find out I want that nigga myself. Oh and find a nigga name Boss we have some business that needs taken care of." I wanted to catch up with Sparkle, but I had bigger issues now.

"Nick come ride with me." When Nick hopped in the car I turned the radio down.

"So who you think dumb enough to cross us?" I asked trying to see where his head was at with the whole situation.

"Yo guess is just as good as mine. That nigga could just be saying shit because he salty we stopped fucking with him on the business tip." I lit the blunt as I listened to my nigga talk. He was making a good point, but I still wanted to be sure.

"So how's my niece bruh?"

"Man her lil ass already spoiled. Tiffany won't put her down, and then when I'm ready to go to sleep her lil ass up crying for somebody to hold her." I smiled thinking about my niece.

"So peep this shit out. When I left your crib looking for Sparkle, I found her and Michael at Denny's. Her ass didn't even let me say shit before she bounced. Michael told me to sit down, and he said that Sparkle is pregnant, but she supposed to be getting an abortion."

"Yo when we were walking to Keeta's crib I heard her confirm an appointment, but didn't think much of it. Do you think that's what the appointment was for?" Nick looked over at me for an answer.

"Bruh I don't even know. When I got done talking to Michael I went to the apartment, and she was in there lights off listening to sad ass music. I go in our room, and she's laying in the bed crying. So I sit at the end of the bed, and she puts the banger to my head." Bruh you lying is all Nick said.

"No but check this shit out I try to plead with her to put it down and she let off a round. That's when y'all niggas called. I was in a fucked up position right now, and needed to figure out how to fix it.

"You hungry nigga cause I need to eat." I asked him pulling up to Fish and Chicken. We got out, and headed in. We ordered our food, and sat down inside to eat. We came up with a game plan on how we were going to handle that nigga Steve.

I knew we had to get him before he got us. Then I told him my plans on dealing with that nigga Boss. After we finished up our food we headed back to the yard to pick up his car.

When I left the yard I hit up the mall. I needed to get me some new clothes since my shit was fucked up. I missed my bitch, but I had to get back to the money. I made a few calls to check on the pill business as well as my guns.

Since I have been so busy with bullshit I had Julio making all runs with my guns, and meeting with potentially new buyers. When it came to my gun empire I was bringing in over two million a year.

Of course Nick was taking care of the pills, and I had Juvy and Roderick being the muscle. I was the voice behind it all. I couldn't focus on nothing while my personal life was fucked up.

Me: Can we meet up?

I needed to get some shit off my chest, and I didn't want it to be done over the phone so I texted Sparkle just to see if she would be willing to hear me out. As bad as I wanted to give her some space I couldn't. No sooner than I put my phone in my pocket it rang. Seeing the name on the screen could have been a good thing, or bad but I had to answer it anyway.

"Yo."

"Can you please meet me?" I heard Meeka crying through the phone. Meeka was my baby sister, and the world stopped when it came to her.

"Yeah meet me at my spot in an hour. I'm about to text you address. I hung up the phone, and texted Meeka the address to me and Sparkle's apartment. I walked out of the mall headed to my car. As soon as I got in and took off I heard a car screeching and the sound of machine guns letting off rounds, but before I could do anything I felt a sharp pain, and everything went black.

To be continued.......

BCPL
Baltimore County
Public Library

CPSIA information can be obtained
at www.ICGtesting.com
Printed in the USA
LVOW12s1723290617
539815LV00002B/404/P